Driving Miss Crazy

Driving Miss Crazy

CONTENTS

BLURB

A mysterious note, a crush-at-first sight, and a plot twist to pull on heartstrings.

It all began with one expertly placed note, smack-dab in the middle of my Zamboni steering wheel:

"Can I have a ride on your Zamboni?
Miss Crazy."

Curiosity gets the best of me, and I have to talk to Miss Crazy.

We text back and forth, exchanging details about our lives, which increasingly become more personal. Come to find out, the person on the phone isn't so crazy at all. She's actually very sweet. We agree to meet up but to my heartbreak, Miss Crazy Person ghosts me.

Everyone says I got played, but I know better.

Something is wrong.

Now, I'm frantic to find out her identity, not only to make sure she's safe, but because not knowing is driving me crazy.

Driving Miss Crazy is a fun novella to introduce you to Mapleton's newest AHL hockey team, Granite Ice. You'll get a glimpse of the world in this sweet read that's meant to be consumed in two-three hours. It has no cliffhangers, a guaranteed HEA, all the swoons, but no explicit scenes.

Introduction

Driving Miss Crazy is a fun novella to introduce you to Mapleton's newest AHL hockey team, Granite Ice. You'll get a glimpse of the world in this sweet read that's meant to be consumed in two-three hours. It has no cliffhangers, a guaranteed HEA, all the swoons, but no explicit scenes. If you love this book, then you'll want to continue with my Sweet Hockey Romcom series already in Kindle Unlimited and ready for you to binge.

You can binge the series here: https://www.amazon.com/dp/B0CWYXGNPL

Happy reading!

One

Sam Summers

"Get a job." My dad's baritone voice foghorns through what should have been a peaceful morning breakfast. Holding his credit card bill in front of his face, he proceeds to run his calloused finger down the long line of my fast-food charges.

Squirming in my seat, I raise my gaze to his. He's always been a hardworking man, living off the land. He's never had much sympathy for people who don't want to work as hard as him. I feel bad for racking up the charges, but what can I say?

I'm a late-night studier.

I need snacks to keep me awake.

Preferably ones with salsa and fresh guac.

I take a moment to set my lukewarm coffee down on the table, the normal temperature since I'm always last to the table in the morning. Some days when I'm really late to the table, I'll give it a quick nuke, but I've gotten so used to it being cooled off by the time I grab it, I prefer it this way. It's a little easier to inch into my day if I don't have to worry about burning my tongue.

Squaring my gaze on him, I move to the edge of my seat, and say, "I've tried to find a job, but nothing works with my schedule." Cough. A tickle bubbles out of nowhere. I ball my hand into a fist and pound on my chest. Okay, that might not be the whole truth.

It's sort of true.

I mean, I pay attention to the Help Wanted signs. I just have never actually left any applications.

"I'm not buying it." Dad shakes his head vehemently as he returns the bill to the table and grabs a strip of crispy bacon. He crunches on the end of it, letting us all hear the ratio of juicy grease and burned edges for a while, before he continues in a confrontational tone, "College kids have been working their way through school for centuries. Your situation is nothing new."

I blank, rewinding his argument as something sounds off. "Centuries?"

"You know what I meant." He waves the bacon at me as if it's a baton. "You're eighteen. I'm fine with you living in my house while you're in college. That doesn't mean you don't have to work. There are no free rides in life. You can at least pay for your own gas and all these tacos."

I cut my gaze to my older sister, Sophie, who is oddly quiet. Poking at her fried eggs with her fork prong, she's content to scroll on her phone with her other hand. I hate to pull her into this argument because it's rare for her to share breakfast with us. She's a famous singer, who lives in town with her husband, Axl, who plays for Mapleton's not-great hockey team. Most of the time, she's out of town for her job, but she's here this week for a charity concert.

After several long beats of my glaring at her for help, she leisurely raises her gaze, offering me a lopsided grin. "It's true. When I was your age, I was already touring and paying all my bills."

"You don't count," I practically growl at her, my heart sliced open in this sibling betrayal. I guess, I can't count on her to stand up for me. I stutter out a rebuttal, "Y-you sing for a living. That's not even a job."

"It doesn't matter what you do, as long as you do something to contribute." Dad's so serious, he props both elbows on the table and leans forward. The old farmhouse table squeaks from his weight, and I hold my breath while he fumes, "You need a job by the end of the day, or I'm taking your credit card back until you get one."

"The end of the day?" I frantically scan the room for my mom, hoping she'll come to my rescue. She's gone somewhere, more than likely to stay out of this conversation. When it comes to my dad, she's not one to take a stance against him. Sweat beads on my brow. This isn't the quiet breakfast I had planned on.

This is life changing!

I'm up against a dead end, and I pull the white flag.

"I'm not against getting a job," I squawk as my throat constricts. "However, it's impossible to get a job by the end of the day."

"This just in." Sophie flashes her phone screen to me. I can barely ignore her cutesy glitter phone case to see what's on her screen. Good thing for me, I don't actually need to focus because she explains everything, "Axl said they are looking for a Zamboni driver at the arena."

"You texted Axl?" My face tightens into a scowl. I don't need Axl weighing in on my life issues. He's all buddy-buddy with my dad. It will only make my dad double down on his ultimatum.

I'm not lazy.

This isn't me trying to get out of responsibility. I just don't want to rush into the first job I see, and I definitely don't want Axl to get me a job. There's no way I can live up to the standard that guy sets. That's always been my issue. Growing up with a famous sister, everyone expects me to shine as bright as her. When they see I'm just ordinary Sam, with no superpowers, their smiles deflate. Most of the time I get the brush-off. It's so insane trying to navigate a path for life when you have a sister who literally can't fail at anything.

When I get a job, I want to do it on my own. I don't want to owe anyone favors, and I don't want to be judged by Axl or Sophie's success. Fighting the urge to hang my head, all I can think is, I'll never measure up.

"Yeah." Sophie's tone is encouraging as she reads from her phone. "He said you don't need any advanced training. He already messaged Cleo, the Head of Arena Maintenance. Cleo said they don't do interviews since it's a labor job. If they like your résumé, and you pass your background check, they give you a trial run to see how you work out. The pay is minimum wage, but you get a discount on concessions. You can stop by tonight to try it out—" she cuts herself off by slamming her gaze toward my dad. "So, he keeps his credit card. He has a job."

"What?" I snap, but that's the only word I can muster. The walls around me seem like they are starting to close in on me. This is not how I planned my day to go! Everything is changing so quickly. Steeling my expression into a stone wall, I challenge her, "There's no way Axl just arranged all that."

Her fingers fly across her phone screen. After a moment of dead silence, she flashes the phone back to me with evidence of a three-way chat between her, Axl, and Cleo.

Cleo's text: Game starts at seven. Have him be here at six.

My hand flies to my forehead, pressure floods to the front of my brain. How did this happen? A moment ago, I was drinking coffee, hardly even awake, and clearly minding my own business. Now I'm employed! "I don't understand how I can secure a job without talking to anyone." I throw out another statement as a last-ditch effort to make this job go away.

"Bill owes me a few favors, and Cleo knows that. In fact, the concert I'm doing this week is basically for Bill's ego. I do a lot of work for that team. Cleo will make it work." Sophie pushes her chair back, flips her dark hair over her shoulder, swipes her empty plate off the table with her other hand, and walks it over to the sink. Then she pivots on her heel, cutting a pointed look toward me. "Just don't make me look bad. Bill is Axl's boss, and he'll make Axl's life miserable if you screw up."

Gulping, I search for my coffee as my throat is parched.

I don't want a pity job.

This won't end well.

I know nothing about driving a Zamboni.

I can't even walk straight.

Why would anyone trust me with one of those massive machines? I chug my coffee all the way to the bottom. *This is going to be a total disaster.* The only thing worse than getting a job right now, is getting a job that Sophie got for me. She's perfect and everyone will be expecting me to be like her.

Staring at the wall, I inhale deep breaths. This better work out. I can only imagine how upset my dad will be if I blow this gig.

One tiny positive thought creeps into my head.

If by slim chance I don't screw this up, I keep my credit card. That means when it's all over, I'll get to indulge in tacos.

For that, I'll do almost anything.

Afterall, how hard can driving a Zamboni be?

Two

Finley Shea

I hate it when my shoe bites me.

I knew better than to wear these fur-trimmed boots after having to stuff my feet into them. But having never been to an ice hockey game before, I was worried about staying warm. It's safe to say, they are a little too snug around the calf. It's not my fault they don't make cute boots for women with larger calves. Now, I'm wincing as I weave my way through the packed Mapleton arena after my sister.

She has a new crush on a hockey player.

I'm not surprised.

It seems Lauren changes crushes as often as she changes her hair color. Every time I see her, there's a new guy she's talking about. I've lost track of how many guys she talked to just this year, but this week she's on a hockey guy kick. I know nothing about him or hockey. Of course, other than what she's told me. This new guy is a recent trade, and he asked her out for tomorrow. She's here to do some "predate investigations."

Since she offered to pay for my way, and supply the popcorn, I'm here. A broke college girl will do what a broke college girl must do to eat. Not to mention, despite our differences, we're close friends. I've always looked up to her and admired her. We've both been so busy lately, we haven't had much time to spend together, just the two of us. I'm looking forward to this time to relax and hang out.

I stop in the center of the steps. Between the hordes of people coming and going in all directions, and the sting in my boot, I'm overwhelmed with walking. "One more row." Lauren nods for me to budge forward. When I don't immediately lift my foot, she tacks on, "Come on, Finley." She lets out one of those sighs that almost sounds like a puke-gag. It's a super disgusting noise. I'd never risk a noise like that. Not in public anyway. People would glare at me. Since she's one of those beautiful girls, she gets away with phlegm-vomit sounds.

Losing her patience, she cuts in front of me, squeezing in between the people already in our row. I stand here, waiting for them to realize that I won't be squeezing in after her.

I hate this part.

Being a curvy girl is largely the main reason I always come early to everything.

The guy at the end of the row looks me up and down, then elbows the guy next to him. One of them emits a raspy grunt, and they both shuffle out of the row, making room for me. My cheeks rage with heat. If they weren't already standing there, with their hands so impatiently tucked in their jacket pockets, waiting on me, I would consider leaving.

"Are you coming?" Lauren huffs out as she's already plopped down in her assigned seat on the other side of the men.

"Sorry," I mutter as I refuse to look either of these guys in the face, and I sidestep all the way to my seat.

Lauren seems oblivious to my sufferings as she spreads her fleece blanket over her chair, taking the oversized edges and wrapping them around her. She's so effortlessly flawless most days.

By most days, I mean every day. I've never seen her not perfect. I love her. I really do. She's a great big sister, but it's impossible for me to feel secure when I'm standing next to her.

I'm a tad sweaty from walking through the whole arena and climbing all those steps. When I plop down, I let out a grunt. It's good to get off my feet. I proceed to shuffle my popcorn and drink against one arm and use my free arm to wipe my brow.

"Okay." Lauren slides to the edge of her seat, craning her neck toward the Granite Ice tunnel. "His name's Elijah. You will know when you see him because he's gorgeous." She sings the last part.

"How can I see him if he has a helmet on?" It's a serious question, as I'm not much of a sports person.

"I'll be sure to point him out." She practically hums from all her excitement. "He's one of the last single guys on the team. It's too bad too because it would be nice if you could find someone to crush on. It will make coming to the games so much more fun."

"The last thing I need is a crush," I murmur as I feed a steady stream of popcorn into my mouth. It's over-oiled popcorn. The kind that leaves the tips of your fingers all greasy. After only a few bites, I forgo wiping them on my pants and lick my fingers one by one.

"It's something to think about for fun." She gives me an encouraging smile. "When's the last time you did something just for fun?"

"I'm here, aren't I?" My brows furrow as I stare back at her. I'm clearly not getting paid to be here. "I don't know another reason I'd come here."

"I thought it was for the food." She gives me a side-eye.

She might have a point.

A half point.

I enjoy the snacks, but I'm cool with the fun part. I waft my gaze forward as a giant bulldozer looking thing comes driving out of the side door and onto the ice. It's massive and floats around like a bristle broom. "What is that?"

"How can you possibly not know what a Zamboni is?" One of her brows quirks, and she glares at me like I've lost my mind. "I mean, I don't know everything about hockey, but I would think you'd have seen one before. They smooth the ice out."

"Sorry, I've never been to a game before. It's not really my scene," I mutter, stealing my gaze on the machine as it takes the corner relatively slowly. The guy driving it has an expression that drifts from scared-for-his-life, all the way to having a blast. He's massively entertaining to watch as he almost clips the goal box. Plus, he's adorable. With dark wavy hair that leaves a stray wispy strand to dangle on his forehead, he isn't hard to look at. "He must be a new guy," I think out loud.

"What?" Lauren looks back at me, the quizzical expression still hasn't left her face.

"That Zamboni driver. He doesn't seem like he knows what he's doing, but he looks like he's having fun."

"Finley." Her words are back with a strong puff of air. "Did you just say you have a crush on the Zamboni driver?"

"Ah, no, I said he looks as if he's having fun." My smile transforms to a scowl. She seems to think the only reason people exist is to pair off into couples.

"That settles it." She exaggeratedly brushes her hands together in front of her like she's accomplished something exhausting. "You can have a crush on him. It's perfect." She swivels in her seat and starts digging in her oversized purse until she whips out a small Post-it pad and a pen.

"What is that for?" A feeling of doom creeps in my chest. One thing about Lauren is that since she's lived her life as one of the pretty "it" girls, she seems to enjoy a special privilege, where life works out her way. Since things work out for her, she does things that most people wouldn't.

"I'm writing him a note," she whispers as she jots down her thoughts. "Hello, Mr. Zamboni Guy. May I have a ride on your Zamboni? Text me at this number if so: 243-3434."

My eyes narrow as I slam my gaze to her paper. She put my real phone number down! "You are not!" I reach over, attempting to swipe the Post-it from her. She pulls it out of my reach, almost smacking the guy on her other side with her elbow.

"It's just for fun." She holds the note over her neighbor's lap. He grimaces but doesn't say anything, and she wouldn't have noticed anyway, because she's still pleading with me, "Fin, he won't even know who wrote it."

"Please." My gaze is pleading. "This is totally juvenile. Seriously, are we in middle school? He's going to think I'm a crazy person."

"Even better." She hums as she quickly lowers the pad and positions her pen above the pad again. "Guys love girls who are a little unhinged. Oh, I got a great idea." She lowers her gaze back to her paper and reads as she writes, "Signed, a crazy person."

I snort-laugh. Nobody will reply to that. I sigh, a deep breath until it fizzles out into another sputter. "Whatever you want to do."

She takes her drink from the cup holder and sips a long pull before shoving it over to me. "Hold my drink. I'm going to try to sneak back there and put this on his seat when he's not watching."

"What—" I start, but she's already weaving her way back through the aisle, marching down the steps with her chin in the air. I want to ask how she intends to just casually slip back to the employee area, but I know the answer.

She's got pretty girl privilege.

Even if she gets caught, she'll just bat her lashes, and she won't get in trouble.

Three

SAM

My palms wash in sweat as adrenaline races through my veins. In a failed attempt to get my nervous sweating at bay, I chugged a ton of water before the game, and I forgot to go to the bathroom. Now, I race to park my Zamboni and kill the engine, hopping down from the cab and hustling through the storage room to find a bathroom. It's super cluttered back here. Shelves line the walls, stacked with spare parts, tools, and other maintenance supplies. With the large Zamboni machine in here, there's hardly any room to move with only one path out. I dart down the hall, all the while replaying how that was one of the coolest things I ever did.

I didn't crash.

I had an hour of training before the game, and Cleo sent me right out. I wasn't expecting that sort of feedback from the fans in the crowd. Apparently, people love Zamboni drivers. Kids even cheered for me.

I was pretty much a superstar out there.

I'm enjoying this gig. It doesn't pay well, but since I didn't get my credit card taken from me, I won't need much. It's an excellent résumé builder, and everyone has to start somewhere. My whole outlook on this job has been transformed. Sure, I didn't want to take any favors from Sophie or Axl, but really, what does it hurt?

When I return to my Zamboni, a woman with an exaggeratedly high, blond ponytail is loitering near my machine. She's wearing an all-black puffer coat, and she has the kind of pouty lips you see on women in makeup commercials.

She's stunning.

She's not wearing Granite Ice gear, which leads me to believe she's not with the team. I'm about to call out to her and ask who she is, but before I can she quickly darts out of the room.

My brow furrows as my gaze follows her. She's in an awful big hurry for some reason.

What if she was up to something?

Nah, I don't know what she could do in the storage room. More than likely she's a fan who got lost. With the height of her ponytail, it doesn't surprise me. She might be losing brain cells from how tight that was. Chuckling, I dismiss her and pace over to examine my machine. Everything looks exactly how I had left it. I must be paranoid. I swipe my brow, noting my palms are growing damp again, even though I just washed them. This job stuff is not for the weak.

Something catches my eye.

A note is taped to the center of my steering wheel. I quickly snatch it up.

"Hello Mr. Zamboni Guy,

May I have a ride on your Zamboni? Text me at this number: 243-3434."

I reread, half thinking this is a joke. When I see that it's signed "Crazy Person," I let out a chuckle.

This is crazy.

I let my gaze drift back out the door. The note came from somewhere. The only person I saw back here was that blonde.

That super stunning blonde who could be a model.

I push my lower lip out, mulling it over. I'm not sure what the policy is on giving people rides as it's only my first day. From what I could tell, she was cute. I stare at her phone number, and ultimately decide, I can't let a pretty girl's number go to waste.

"Why not?" I say out loud as I dig in my pocket for my phone. "I don't have anything better to do."

I text: **Hey, Crazy Person. About your request, I'm not sure about the ride policy. This is my first day. I'll have to ask my boss.**

It takes only a minute for the text to be marked seen, and I get another one back.

Crazy Person: That explains so much.

Confusion sets in, and my brows dip. What explains so much?

Crazy Person: You're a terrible driver.

Anger bubbles in my gut, and I spout back: **Am not. There's a learning curve, and I'd like to see you jump on one of those things.**

Crazy Person: I'm trying to. That's why I asked.

A shuffling comes from around the door, and Cleo strides over. I quickly stuff my phone in my pocket, focusing my attention on him. "What's up?"

"I was looking for you." Cleo's dressed in a faded navy-blue uniform shirt that matches his pants and has his name stitched onto a patch on the chest. His face is weathered and lined, but he's not grumpy-looking. If anything, the lines on this face extend his smile. He nods behind him. "We have seats right out there for you to watch the game. You don't have to sit back here the whole time. The periods take a while."

"Right, I know that." I turn toward him, dragging my feet. I don't mind hockey. I've been to an awful lot of games since Axl's become one of our family members, but I'm struggling with first-day flutters.

Puckering his brow, he asks, "What were you doing anyway?"

Before I can consider how it's going to sound, I blurt out, "I was just talking to a crazy person."

He laughs a deep laugh from low in his gut. "Aren't we all?"

Four

FINLEY

I cover my mouth, suppressing a squeal as Lauren and I race out of the arena. I'm in a hurry to get out of here, before Mr. Zamboni sees me. "I can't believe he texted us back," I shriek once I step outside, and we sprint toward my car. It's always freezing in Mapleton this time of year. Since we had been sitting in an arena for three hours, you'd think we'd be used to the cold.

There's still a drastic dip in temps.

I want to run, as that is my goal, but my feet are pinched inside these boots. I've been suffering all night, and I resort to a hop-skip-gallop pattern.

Anything to lessen the pain.

"Well, of course he replied." Lauren effortlessly jogs next to me. Her poise is too perfect with her elevated chin. She pumps her arms at her side, as if she is out for a Sunday stroll. She's not even breathing heavily.

I break out into a wheezing cough before I even make it to my car. I've never been tested for asthma. It's times like these I think I should be. I suck in as much air as I can, while I wind my speed down to a halt and eagerly slip into the already warm and running car. I take a minute to rub my hands together, and my phone beeps right as I shift the car into drive.

"I got it." Lauren grapples for my phone. She masterminded my earlier text to Mr. Zamboni. If I had replied, I would have deleted them without reading them. I stare at her as she reads the text out loud.

Mr. Zamboni: About Zamboni rides, I need to learn to drive it better first. Sorry, but I think it's going to be a no for now.

I wish I had her confidence because she doesn't even pause as she holds the phone in front of her and boldly reads what she texts back:

I'll take that raincheck. When you are ready for rides, I want to be the first one.

"Give me my phone." I have one eye on her as I struggle to focus on steering out of the arena parking lot. "I don't want to get him in trouble."

"He's not going to get in trouble. He's driving a Zamboni, not doing brain surgery." Her lips whoosh to the side, and my stomach drops.

I know that expression.

That's her thinking-about-trouble look.

"Please, it's getting out of hand. It was funny in there, but he's probably a nice guy, who doesn't deserve to be harassed." I take a left, and a horrid thought enters my brain. I immediately spew it out, "What if he has a girlfriend?"

"It's called flirting. Certainly not harassment. If you don't know that, then you need to have more of it. Plus, if he has a girlfriend, then he has an obligation to say so," she says as I give her a side-eye. She lifts my phone again and says, "I'll ask him."

My cheeks rage with an inferno fire. I don't even know why. It's dark in the car. No one can see me. I'm not used to flirting or whatever this is. "Please, leave it alone."

"No girlfriend or wife," she proudly reports. "Single and ready to mingle."

"That's what he said?"

"Well, I made up the ready to mingle part, but why would he be texting you if he isn't?" Her gaze drops to my phone. "So, Mr. Zamboni," she says as she types. "What do you like to do after work to relax?"

I steer onto the highway, setting my cruise as she reads his reply, "I volunteer at the local animal shelter."

"What?" I drop my jaw, as there is no way he's not joking. "That can't be real?"

"Yeah, it sounds like he's trying to be playful." She reads as she types, "No way you do that. That's just what you tell all the girls to try to impress them. Isn't it?"

"We should get tacos." My stomach rumbles right as I say it. I'm already smelling garlic and cilantro off-gassing from the take-out bag I don't have yet.

"We just ate." Lauren drops my phone back to her lap, jerking her gaze over to me as if I said something incriminating.

"Not really." I squeeze the steering wheel. I wonder what it would be like to not enjoy food. "I ate popcorn at the game, and it was three hours long. How can you go without food?"

My phone lights up, and Lauren quickly retrieves it, holding it closer to her face as she reads, "Well, not all the girls. Just you. Did it work?" Her eyebrows shoot to the sky. "Oh! He's definitely flirting with you! Did you hear that?"

"No, he's flirting with you." A chuckle braids with my words as I shake my head.

"He doesn't know that." Her fingers fly across my phone again. "I'm helping you get started because you're too modest. It's basically an introduction."

"The longest introduction ever." I give her another side-eye.

"We still have to drive back to town, which takes a few minutes. What else am I supposed to be doing?" She tosses up her shoulder and keeps texting.

"Oh, I don't know. We could talk between ourselves."

"What do you want to talk about?" Her voice feels distant, like how my mom used to try to appease my questions when she was busy trying to do something else.

I want to ask her about school. It's my freshman year of college, and I feel so lost. I have no idea what I should major in, and the time is going fast. She never seemed to struggle with that stuff. She got through school, making it seem like it was a never-ending fashion show. Now, she spends her days in a cushy law office working as a paralegal. None of it seems to faze her. Her toughest decision is what pencil skirt to wear. She's just so poised and not . . . not like me. She won't understand what I'm feeling. "Ah, well, all this talk about Mr. Zamboni, and you haven't said one word about that hockey player." I go with something safe that she'll care about. "Are you over your crush so soon?"

"Oh, no." She looks around, finding my boho-style purse in the center console, where she takes a moment to tuck my phone back as if nothing was going on at all. If I had known all it took for her to stop texting that guy was for me to ask her about the hockey guy, I would have done that immediately. "I still like him. I just had business to take care of."

She's still speaking, but I zone out. For sisters, we certainly don't have much in common—if anything. I don't think about the stuff she talks about. And my stomach rumbles again, asking for a taco.

Call me crazy for needing to eat, but I know what I'm doing as soon as I drop her off.

Arriving to my dorm room with a snack sack, I'm thankful to be alone. I'm one of the lucky freshmen who got a single room. It's the only reason I haven't gone crazy. I'm not anti-social at all. I'm selectively social. Spending all day in classes, and then extra socializing like tonight's hockey game, wears me out. I drop my purse and my Ted's Tacos bag on my desk, and I attempt to slip off my boots.

They aren't slipping.

In fact, they aren't even budging. My ankles are puffed up, and everything is so tight. I drop my butt to my desk chair and yank with both hands. They come off with a heave. Out of breath, I lazily toss them next to my desk as I make a mental note to never wear them again. I'm sticking to my Crocs in sport mode—even when it snows. They make socks for those days.

I chuckle, as I know it's absurd.

Comfort at all costs.

I shift my taco bag to the side, making room for my homework, and retrieve my psychology book. It's the only subject I'm taking this semester that's even a little interesting.

I still won't say I like it.

"There," I breathe out, as I prepare for an hour of studying. I reach in the taco bag and inhale the deepest breath I can.

It's heaven in a sack.

In my peripheral, my phone's lighting up in my purse.

It's got to be Lauren.

Setting my taco down, careful to keep all the chicken neatly tucked inside, I snatch my phone and immediately suck in a breath.

I have several unread texts from Mr. Zamboni that I didn't even know about. I scroll up. Lauren texted all sorts of things without telling me.

Me: What's your favorite movie to cuddle to?

My hand flies to cover my slack jaw. She asked him that! Boy, that's not even playing a little hard to get. My heart rams against my chest, as I read on.

Mr. Zamboni: Anything horror.

Me: Those aren't cuddle movies.

Mr. Zamboni: Are you kidding me? They are the definition of cuddle movies. What's yours?

Me: Well, lately I've been bingeing British soap operas.

Ah! I dramatically stand, my jaw drops even farther to the floor. She told him that! That's the private obsession I told her about in confidence. She doesn't need to tell people that. My eyes are practically throbbing as I read on.

Mr. Zamboni: Haha. Like those PBS ones?

Me: Yes, those are my jam.

Now I want to throw up. Who says jam? She's making me out to be a nerd. Okay, maybe I love those shows a little.

I don't tell people that. At least not strangers!

My stomach sinks to a whole new level as I fight with the urge to shut my phone off and never think about this again.

However, I'm nosy...

I must see what else she said.

Mr. Zamboni: You asked me if I had a girlfriend, I'm assuming you don't have a boyfriend.

Me: I've never had one.

I'm dead.

I drop my phone to my desk, heaving myself on my bed in one fell swoop. Why would she tell him that? That's sacred knowledge, and she just threw it out there in a text. I want to pick up my phone to call her and scream at her, but then I have to look at my phone. The very thought is making me nauseous.

On perfect cue, it lights up from its spot on my desk.

Oh man...

Whimpering, I inch off my bed and stare at my phone, dread consuming me. There's a reason curiosity killed the cat. With my eyes clenched, I slip my phone back off my desk and slide it in front of my face. I must know what he said.

Mr. Zamboni: Oh, really? How come?

Me: I haven't found anyone who loves tacos as much as I do.

I smile when I read Lauren's reply. It's partially true. Anyone I date is going to need to love tacos. Then I read on.

Mr. Zamboni: Haha. You love tacos? That's my favorite food. I literally have them every night.

This is where Lauren must have stopped replying, because it's just a few texts from Mr. Zamboni:

Do you like the ones from Ted's Tacos? They are my favorite.

Mr. Zamboni: I'm going to run there right now. I like extra spicy salsa.

Mr. Zamboni: What do you like?

Phew. I let out the breath I was holding. Well, at least he didn't freak out when he heard I never had a boyfriend. I'm glad that's over. I drop back to my seat and set my phone above my book, out of reach, turning my attention to my tacos.

I chuckle. That's so weird we both stopped for Ted's Tacos. What are the odds?

I mean, they are really good tacos. Ted's is always busy, but it seems ironic.

Casually, I glance around my room as if I'm half-expecting someone to be there looking over my shoulder. Man, I love living by myself. Would it really hurt to text him back my taco order? He's literally texting tacos. It's like my love language. Lauren would have fired a text back right away without thinking. She's a natural flirt. I overthink things too much. A sly smile creeps on my lips. I roll my bottom lip under my top teeth as I reach for my phone. Why not?

Me: That's so funny. I just stopped there too. I love anything from Ted's Tacos, but I got the chicken soft shell tonight.

He replies!

Mr. Zamboni: You can't ever go wrong with their chicken.

I drop my phone back to my desk. This is absurd. Why am I texting a stranger?

Another text quickly comes in.

Mr. Zamboni: Is it just me, or do they taste even better the closer it gets to midnight?

I don't even think about what to say as that's a no-brainer. I shoot back:

For sure. They must have a flavor meter that dials up after dinner.

Mr. Zamboni: Haha! You're too funny. You made me laugh out loud.

A smile tugs on the corners of my lips, and I bite the inside of my cheek as I reread his reply. It feels good to chat. He seems like he has an easygoing personality. The quibbles in my gut slowly even out as I construct another text.

Me: It might be biology. Like, our brain receptors for tacos fire more rapidly after the sun goes down.

Mr. Zamboni: LOL Right! We must have tacos to manage our mental health.

Me: Totally. It's so much better than drinking.

Mr. Zamboni: You don't party?

I stop. Lauren always says I don't have a fun personality, because I've never been into that. I don't dance or go out. I'd definitely rather have tacos in private than anything in public, but again, it's not one of those things I tell people.

Me: Naw. What about you? Do you go out much?

Mr. Zamboni: Never. I'm a homebody. If it wasn't for having to work, I would never have been at that hockey game.

My brows shoot up. I love his response. He's exactly like me. Now, I can't type fast enough.

Me: Same! I only went tonight because my sister drug me out. I don't even remember what happened at the game. Well, other than when I saw you.

Mr. Zamboni: Haha. You mean to tell me I distracted you so much with my Zamboni skills, you didn't watch an entire hockey game?

Me: Yeah.

I'm smiling so large now, my heart ticks up a notch. He seems sweet. This isn't as scary as I thought it would be. Not when you get over the first part, and we have things in common.

Mr. Zamboni: What are you doing now?

Me: Well, texting you and going to start eating my taco before it gets cold. What about you?

Mr. Zamboni: Same.

Who would think two people could form a taco bond so fast, but it's what's happening. We spend the next almost hour, texting all things taco, school, living in Mapleton, and a whole lot of randomness. I'm giddy with giggles by the time I finally pull myself away from my phone and force myself to study.

Mr. Zamboni is adorable.

Five

SAM

My eyes spring wide awake, and the first thing I think about is tacos. Then my thoughts quickly avert to Miss Crazy. She's fun to talk to. I've never met a woman who wants to talk about tacos as much as me.

She's like my soul mate.

Most of the women I talk to are obsessed with fashion and makeup. I can't talk for long about that stuff before I get quiet and end up doing all the listening. Then I get blamed for being shy. I'm not shy around women.

I'm mostly bored of them.

But not her.

I quickly reach for my phone and shoot off a text.

Me: Good morning, Crazy Person.

Maybe it's too early to text? Maybe I'm obsessed? I stare at my phone, and a smirk forms on my lips as soon as I see:

Crazy Person: That's Miss Crazy to you.
Oh, she's feisty today.
Me: Got it, Miss Crazy. What are you doing today?
Miss Crazy: I have class at 8. U?
Me: Same. Well, I have class at 9. Can I text you later?
Miss Crazy: Sure :P

Today is going to be a great day. I just know it. I jump out of bed and whistle through my morning routine. There's an extra pep in my step when I enter the kitchen. Dad's at the table eating bacon by himself as Sophie's back at her house today.

"Morning." I open the pantry, scanning for something that catches my eyes. French toast bagels. Yum. I retrieve a bagel, and pop it into the toaster. While it's toasting, I grab the peanut butter and a knife, and ready my plate.

"I didn't even hear you come in last night. How was work?" Dad peers at me over his phone, where he reads the morning news.

"It was good." I nod and then nod again when I can't think of anything to complain about. "Yeah, I'm going to like it. Cleo, my boss, thinks if I want extra hours, I might be able to pick some up doing event setup and things."

"That sounds good." Dad's lower lip pushes out, tipping me off he's got something to add, and I wait. "Good for you, Son."

Seriously? My head jolts back. Did he just sort of compliment me?

That's a first.

"Thanks?" It comes out more like a question. My bagel is done to the perfect crunchy perfection. I snatch it out of the toaster, taking a moment to smooth peanut butter on it.

Dad stands, scooting his chair back with a screech across the floor. "Do you work tonight?"

"They don't need anyone, but Cleo said if I want to stop in to meet the other Zamboni guy, I can. He thought it might be good for me to shadow and see if I can pick up some more tips."

"That's a good idea." Dad moves his plate to the sink, rinsing it before putting it in the dishwasher. "Well, let me know when your next game is, and I'll put it on my calendar to come watch."

"Sure." I'm quieter than usual. My dad has never been the guy who comes to watch me do things. That might be partially because I don't do much. A tinge in my chest buds as I think about his offer. *It feels...amazing.*

Taking both halves of my bagel, I smash it together and watch as the peanut butter oozes out the side. *Mouthwatering perfection.* Then I bite off a good chunk as I move toward the door and slip on my sandals. Never mind that it's cold out. I hate tying my shoes. I'd rather have a little discomfort from the cold air while I walk to class than waste time tying my shoes. Plus, it's good for my health to wear sandals in the winter. I walk much faster, which is excellent exercise. I bet if I even mentioned this hack at my next checkup, it would be doctor approved.

After class, I speed to my car just enough to get my heart rate up to optimal levels. Not that I know what level it should be. I'm not a fitness guru of any sort. I just tell myself this as I whip out my phone to text Miss Crazy.

I don't resist the smile on my face.

Me: How was your day, Miss Crazy?

Miss Crazy: Cold. Especially since I wore Crocs.

What?

My eyes bug out from my head. Did I read that right? I'm so excited to know more about this, I immediately shoot off a text.

Me: Seriously? I wore sandals because I hate tying shoes. Do you hate it too?

Miss Crazy: No, I don't hate tying them, but I find most shoes uncomfortable. I prefer slip-on shoes.

This woman is after my heart. I can't even handle the way my chest inflates, filling so full of all the feels. I didn't know women like this existed.

Me: So, let me get this straight. We both love tacos and can't stand shoes. It sounds like we just invented our perfect first date. Barefoot with tacos.

Miss Crazy: I love it!

My heart slams against my rib cage. I can't wait to meet her. I don't put it off for another second. Still, I need to play it cool...

Me: I'm stopping by the arena later tonight to train with the other Zamboni guy. Do you want to come when I'm done, and I'll give you a spin, and then we can go for tacos?

Holding my hand on my heart, I wait for her to text back. It's an extra-long pause. I hope it's not intentional, because I'm not a guy who plays games. Not about tacos.

Miss Crazy: Sure. What time?

My heart backflips and then kicks so hard I almost stumble. I stop walking as I stare at my phone. This is amazing. Ah, what time? I have no idea. This is my first job.

Me: Can I text you later when I know how long it will take? I'm not real sure.

Miss Crazy: That's perfect.

Me: Deal. I can't wait to see you again.

I'm about to tuck my phone into my coat pocket but it quickly vibrates.

Miss Crazy: What do you mean see me again?

I smile as I recall how I saw her sneak away from my Zamboni.

Me: I saw you leave after you put that note on my Zamboni. I mean, not really good, but I noticed how you had long blond hair and were wearing that black jacket. You're beautiful.

I pause and reread my text before I send it. I've never outwardly told a woman she's beautiful. Miss Crazy seems sweet, and I don't feel shy saying that. I feel like we are building a strong foundation of mutual love of sandals and tacos. I chuckle to myself as I get that sounds absurd, but it feels right. I press send.

I'm in my car now, and I slip inside. No other text comes. She's more than likely busy. I'll text her later. I can't help but smile my biggest smile yet as I start my car and pull out. To the arena, where my Zamboni awaits...

Six

FINLEY

This is bad.

I stare at my text, rereading it over and over. Each time my heart sinks lower and lower.

This is beyond bad.

This is absolutely the worst thing that can happen.

How did I not figure this out sooner?

Mr. Zamboni saw Lauren.

He thinks I'm her!

You might as well stab me in the heart with a dagger. Okay, that's extreme, but if he's seriously expecting Lauren... he's going to throw up when he sees me. Panicking, I dial Lauren and pace my room until she answers.

"Hey, Fin."

"You never told me Mr. Zamboni saw you drop off that note!"

"Ah, I didn't know he did. Why? What happened?"

"Well, we made plans to meet up tonight. I was really look-ing forward to it, but then he made some comment about how he couldn't wait to see me *again*. At first, I thought it was a typo. I decided to ask him about it. He said he saw you drop off that note. Do you know what this means?"

"Um, it means he saw me."

"It means he's expecting *you*."

"Ah, no." Her tone waivers between following along and slightly confused. "If he made plans with you, he's expecting you."

"Lauren," I plead, not because I'm trying that hard to get her to understand. She'll eventually catch up. I plead because it's not fair. The one time I meet someone who I think I could like, and he's already prepped for a huge letdown. "It's one thing if he is expecting to meet an average-looking woman, but Lauren, you make Barbie look average. Plus, I'm not av-erage. I'm a solid three. Maybe. On a good day. Okay, maybe a four if I wear cute shoes. We both know I hate wearing cute shoes, so that hardly ever happens."

"Okay, you can stop with the self-deprecation. If I didn't think he was a good match for you, I would have never set this up. You have an amazing personality."

"We both know he's not expecting a good personality."

"What does that mean?" Her volume is softer.

"You know." My volume grows more somber too. This is one of those things that is hard to explain to people like Lauren. When she walks into a room, everyone turns toward her. The only way I turn heads is if I accidentally make a giant commotion.

"Well, give him a chance to get to know you a little first," she goes on. "Didn't you text him? I thought he was super sweet."

"I did text him." I let out a huff that borders on a whimper. "He is sweet." That's the hardest part to come to terms with. I never want to talk to anyone, but he is one person I'd love a chance to see in person and get to know better. Thanks to Lauren, unfortunately, this meeting will never happen.

"Just tell him that was your sister." Her tone is matter of fact. "He'll understand."

"Will he?" Anger bubbles into my gut. "Because if you say sister, most people think I'd be like another version of you, only in a slightly different hue. We are total opposites."

"How do you know he even cares what you look like?" she drones on, only making my stomach knot tighter.

"Because he said I was beautiful." My voice cracks as I squeeze the last word out. I've never been called beautiful before.

"You're making too big of a deal out of this, just like you make too big of a deal out of most things. Just go meet him.

Have dinner or whatever you want to do. If you don't hit it off, no big deal."

"Easy for you to say. You've never had to see the look on people's faces when they meet me, after they've met you..." I should have known better than explaining this to Lauren. I'm not trying to wallow in self-pity. I do believe I could be a good partner to the right person. That's not going to happen this time. "I better go."

I end the call and open my text message, taking time to reread the last part over and over.

You're beautiful.

Shaking my head, tears well in my eyes, but I do what I need to do—delete his text. There's no way I'm going to even bother showing up. I can imagine his scowl when he sees me.

Seven

SAM

After the game, I park my machine and stand next to my Zamboni. I can't wait an extra second to text Miss Crazy.

Me: I'm done and free for the rest of the night. How are things on your end?

I press send and stare at my phone. I don't get a text back right away.

It's okay. She might need time to notice it. I'm not proud of it, but I clear my throat and practice my deep voice. "Hello."

That sounds so dumb.

More casual. Less throat.

Swallowing, I revert to my normal tone, "Hello."

"Hello!" Cleo's voice slices through the air. I startle and stand in attention like I have some weird military thing going on with my legs.

"Aw, hey," I squeak and then shake my head in horror. I haven't squeaked since I made it out this end of puberty. I've never been so nervous to meet someone before. All this buildup is making me senseless.

"How did it go?" Cleo strides over, taking a moment to look around my Zamboni. "Everything looked good on my end."

"I think I'm getting the hang of it." I nod, placing my hand on the machine, giving it a little pat. "She's sure fun to drive."

"Just wait until the ladies start noticing." He stuffs his hands in his jacket and rocks back on his heels with one of those expressions that says he knows something. "These machines are lady catchers."

"Oh, yeah?" I squeak again. What is wrong with me? I'm certainly not going to confess I already found this out to be true. I wasn't looking to meet any women.

It was an accident.

A happy accident, like serendipity.

"Oh, for sure." He scans the room quickly and then flicks his gaze back to me. "Well, if you don't have any questions or anything, I'm going to take off for the night. Make sure all the lights are shut off before you leave."

"Sounds good." I nod right as he turns on his heel, and I wait for him to leave before I check my phone.

No text.

This is odd. She knew I was going to text her. Maybe I should have been more specific on the time? Hopefully, she doesn't think I took too long.

Would it be okay if I called?

Calling seems desperate.

I'll send another text.

Me: Hey, me again. I'm all done here, but totally fine waiting if you are busy. Let me know what time works for you. Do you want to come here? Or would you rather meet for tacos?

I press send. Then I quickly reread it.

That sounds dumb.

I shoot off another text for damage control.

Me: Haha. So excited to see you. Can't you tell? We don't have to do tacos if there is something else you want to do. I'm down for whatever.

I wait a few minutes. No text comes back. It's clearly because I'm staring at my phone like waiting for a pot of hot water to boil. I chuckle and stuff my phone in my pocket while I start to pace. Lifting my chin, I look around as I whistle and start to make laps. She'll be texting back any minute.

After the second lap, I can't stand the suspense, and I yank my phone out and text:

Me: Just checking that we had plans. Maybe I was confused. I thought we were going to meet up. I'm cool with whatever.

Yeah, I'm sure she's getting ready for our date. I know how girls are. They take forever to get ready. Judging by the way she looked last night, I'm sure she'll be just as beautiful. I don't mind one bit... I pace around.

And around.

After another five minutes, I text: **So, I'm wrapping things up and heading out for tacos. You're welcome to join me.**

A smile takes over my face now. She loves tacos as much as I do. She'll be texting right back.

I whistle some more, walking a little faster as I leave the arena and hustle to my car. The windshield is frosted over, and I take a moment to scrape it. Then I get in the car, whipping my phone out of my pocket because I surely missed her text.

Nothing.

What is going on?

My phone must be frozen. I open my contacts, pressing send on Sophie's name. It immediately goes into a call, and she picks up. "Hello."

"Soph," I rush out, speaking loudly. "Can you hear me?"

"Yes." Her words are exaggeratedly spaced. "I. Can. Hear. You. Why?"

"My phone wasn't working but it must have just started." I pull it away from my ear and scan it. It looks the same. Putting the phone back to my ear, I say, "Well, I guess it's working. Thanks."

"Why would you think it's not working?" Sophie chuckles. In the background I hear her husband, Axl, asking what's going on. She whispers to him, "Sam thought his phone was broken." There's so much background noise I have a hard time making out their conversation.

"I had this date planned for tonight," I go on. "I've texted her at least five or ten times, and she hasn't replied. I'm sure it will be fine now that my phone works. Where are you at? It's super loud there."

"We had dinner at Red Barn with Axl's new teammate tonight. It's sort of a double date. Sam." Her tone is extra curt as she changes the subject. "Have you seriously never been stood up before?"

"Wait. What?" My brows furrow together, and my thoughts ramble out, "What do you mean stood up? How would that happen?"

"Your phone is working fine. Evidence is you're talking to me. You were ghosted." One would think since she's my sister, she'd be a little empathetic, but she's more chuckling than anything. "Don't worry," she adds after I'm too speechless to say anything. "It happens to everyone."

"I don't think that's true." I'm back to squeaking. "We had so much in common, and we were going to eat tacos. I just need to text her one more time to see if she's even getting my texts."

"Sam." Now she has an empathetic tone. "Do yourself a favor and let it go now. It's nothing personal. It happens to everyone."

"I didn't get ghosted." It's my turn to rush out laughing. "Thanks for caring though. Now that my phone is working, I'm going to text her before it gets late. Bye."

I end the call, shaking my head. Sophie has the wildest ideas.

I open my text messages. Still no text. I'm sure my phone needs to sync or something.

Me: Hey, it's me. Sorry, but my phone wasn't working. It's so weird. Now it is. So, if you get a bunch of messages from me at once, that's why. Anyway, I'm headed out from work and still going to stop for tacos and would LOVE to see you.

I send the text and set my phone on the dash with the screen up. Then I pull my car forward with my gaze cutting to my phone every other second. I make it all the way to Ted's Tacos—a fourteen-minute drive, and no text.

I grab my phone and stare at all my messages. They show they were all received. How can it be?

Was I seriously ghosted?

My heart sinks like a hundred-pound anchor is pulling it down. I've never had this happen before. I hate this feeling.

Why wouldn't she at least let me know she changed her mind?

Was it all a joke?

Anger bubbles in my gut. No. I shake my head. She wouldn't have texted me for an hour last night for a laugh. Would she?

Hovering my thumb over my phone, I wrestle with the want to text her again, to ask her why she did this. All she had to do was say she wasn't interested.

I should have deleted her name and did what Sophie told me to do. Let it go now. I had one more question for her.

Me: I get it. You're not coming. Can I at least know your real first name?

She's not going to answer now. Who knows, maybe she is deleting everything as she gets it. I stuff my phone in my pocket and go inside the taco shop to order a LOT of tacos to eat...alone.

Fuming, I order a twelve-pack. On any other day, twelve tacos all to myself would be bliss. I don't want to eat them alone. My heart is literally pulsating against my chest. I'm so upset, I could scream. When I get my taco sack, I hurry outside and do a double take. The truck I'm parked behind looks like Axl's.

Oh, wait. I practically stumble over my own feet to stop dead in my tracks.

Sophie said they were at Red Barn. I'm just down the block. My gaze wafts forward and without thinking I stride that way. I'll stop for a minute while I eat. I slip inside the restaurant and good thing for me, it's past peak dinner hours. There's no hostess waiting by the door. Having been here tons of times, I know exactly where to go. They always sit at the high-top 'tables next to the bar. I walk straight ahead until I see them.

First, I spot Sophie. She's wearing a Granite Ice sweatshirt and laughing at something. Her gaze quickly pulls to mine and her smile fades. "Sam. What are you doing here?"

"Hey, guys." I pull up a barstool without being asked. I'm not usually like this. It must be the shock of everything, but I just have this strong desire to not be alone right now. "I was next door getting tacos and saw your truck. If it's okay, I thought I'd say hi." Without waiting for an invitation, I reach in my taco sack and pull out one and hand it to Axl, who is sitting next to me. "Taco?"

"I don't think you can bring outside food in here." He looks over his shoulder but takes it anyway. A rascal smile plants on his lips as he begins to unwrap it. Everyone I know is obsessed with these tacos. You can never say no to them. I knew it would help soothe my crashing their dinner.

"What are they going to do? Kick me out?" I offer a weak laugh and retrieve another taco and hand it to Sophie. "I got way too many tacos. You guys must help me eat these."

I reach in the sack as there are two more people sitting at the table. Axl jerks his thumb over his shoulder toward the gentleman sitting next to him. "Have you met Elijah yet? He's the trade on our team."

"No." Instead of offering a handshake, I pass his taco to him. "Nice to meet you. Have a taco." He quirks a fuzzy eyebrow at me and holds my gaze for a moment as he stays a little frozen. I get this looks weird, but I'm desperately trying to fit in.

"Thanks?" His facial expression flashes perplexion, but I still don't feel bad crashing their dinner. I'm only planning to stay a little while. There's another person sitting at the table. I reach back into the sack and grab another taco. "Nice to meet—" I cut myself off when I lift my gaze and freeze.

High blond ponytail.

Pouty lips that should come with a warning label.

Lovely big blue eyes that squint slightly from the way she's smiling at me. And a body with so many curves, it looks like it should only know how to move in slow motion. Now I want to fall over. "You!" I scream and point my foil-wrapped taco at her.

"Me?" she startles, tossing a look behind her. Actually, everyone at the table startles.

Sophie drops her hand to my arm, giving it a more than a gentle squeeze. "Sam, what's going on?"

"Her!" I point my taco at her again. I'm unable to get my sentences out. "Her. I don't know her name, but she ghosted me." I suddenly notice I'm wagging my taco around like a crazy person and dramatically drop it back in my sack. "She cannot have a taco! She missed her chance."

"Sam." Sophie squeezes my arm again, dropping her volume, "You're acting like a crazy person."

"She's the crazy person! She even told me that's her name."

Axl flashes an apologetic look to Miss Crazy. "Do you know Sam?"

"Not at all." She wags her head, her eyes swelling large.

"Sure you don't." I push my chin up and study this whole situation from an angle. She's clearly on some date with this hockey guy. That's why she couldn't meet up with me. Wait until he hears that she has been texting me the last two days. I yank out my phone to reveal all the evidence and see a new text message from Miss Crazy. "Oh look," I say haughtily. "Looks like you finally messaged me back." I click on the text and see she answered my question.

Miss Crazy: My name is Finley.

And her name pings me in the heart like a dagger. Of course, she has a beautiful name to go with that beautiful face.

"Is your name Finley?" I'm acting like a complete tool but don't care. All the eyes around the table are staring at me. My give-a-care is broken.

"It's Lauren." She's calm as she stares back, blinking once and then adds, "Finley is my sister. How do you know her?"

Oh no!

Now, I've done it.

"You have a twin?" I gasp. "I'm so sorry. I've just completely made a jerk of myself. I was supposed to meet your twin—" Now I'm fumbling around for something to fidget with. I don't even have a glass of water.

Man, it's hot in here.

I crack the top of my jacket zipper open. That does nothing to help. I stuff my hand back in my sack. It's dead silent with all eyes on me when I yank out another taco and present it to her. "Here. Sorry. Have a taco now."

"Sam." Sophie leans forward, urgent eyes trapping me. Her brows are lifted all the way to her widow's peak. "Tell me the truth. I won't tell Mom. Have you been drinking?"

"No." My mind is blown. There's nothing left but a big giant sac of air in my head. I look to Lauren, back to her date, and then to Sophie. "I just made a fool out of myself."

"Yeah, you did," Sophie asserts as she pats my arm gingerly. "But tell me what's going on anyway, and I'll try to help you. How do you know Lauren's sister?"

"Yeah." Lauren perks up, turning her attention to me.

"I don't know her, but she started texting me yesterday. We were going to meet up—"

I stop talking because Lauren's eyes round even more like she made a connection. "Are you Mr. Zamboni?"

"Ah, yes, I have been driving a Zamboni, just since yesterday."

Her nod is slow at first, and then gradually she picks up more speed. "Yes. I know what this is all about."

"At least one of us does." I lift one side of my lips into a lopsided grin, even though I'm not feeling the least bit smiley. More like hopeless, confused, and humiliated. "Care to fill me in?"

"I can." Her gaze wafts around the table, and her voice drops. "Let's go for a walk outside. It's a little sensitive."

My heart slams against my rib cage. I can't handle any more shock tonight. I get up from the table and tuck my taco sack back into my arm. "Sure, we'll walk, talk, and taco."

Eight

Finley

Staring at my algebra book, I will my eyes not to go cross-eyed. One thing about me is that although I don't know what I want to do with my life, I know whatever it is does not involve algebra. The alphabet has no business encroaching into the numbers system. They each have perfectly fine systems on their own.

A shuffle outside my door distracts my attention, but I ignore it. It's quickly followed by a knock. The only person who comes to see me is Lauren, but she has her date tonight. "Who is it?" I'm generally perplexed as I rise to my feet and cross the narrow room.

It's so odd. If I didn't know better, I would say I'm smelling garlic and chili seasoning with a sprinkle of cumin. I don't remember ordering Door Dash. Following the scent to my door, I crack it open enough to push my nose through.

It's cilantro, paprika, and if I'm not mistaken a hint of—*Mr. Zamboni!*

My brows shoot to the ceiling, and I freeze on his face. I'd only seen him once. Yes, it was from a distance, but I did not forget his face. Chiseled cheekbones and piercing blue eyes. His thick eyebrows are perfectly arched, framing his symmetrical face. All in all, his face is proportioned in the perfect way, and that's before we get to his full lips. He looked good from a distance, but up close is no comparison.

"Finley?" There's a slight rasp in his tone that sends a shiver directly down my spine. My cheeks immediately heat when he stares back at me.

Coming face-to-face with this gorgeous man would be hard under any circumstances. With my mind stuck on the fact he's not expecting me, I'm speechless. I only nod a yes.

Shifting his weight from one leg to the other, he does nothing else to indicate he's uncomfortable or upset. I wait for the look of horror to flash across his face, but he tips one side of his full lips into a lopsided grin. "Uh, sorry to barge in on you like this. I can explain."

"I can explain," I rush out as I find my voice.

"No." He raises his palm, flashing a gentle stop motion. "Let me go first."

"Okay." Should I just stand here? I really don't need to be yelled at for something that was never my fault. Maybe if he's really upset, he'll storm out of here. Then I won't have to explain. I cross my arms over my chest and fix my attention on him, which is hard to do since he has a Ted's Taco bag tucked in the crook of his arm. It's a tad distracting.

"I got your address from your sister, Lauren."

"My sister?" I tip my head toward him and replay his sentence. This already isn't making sense. "How?"

"I ran into her on her date tonight. I sorta went a little crazy thinking she ghosted me, but she explained everything to me. I'm so sorry for the mix-up."

"Wait." I blink and then blink again. "You're sorry?"

"Yeah, I should have never assumed that Lauren was you, and I get how that made you feel awkward…" He shakes his head, sorrow etched on his face. "I was nervous about meeting you too. For what it's worth, I would love to start fresh."

In my heart, I'm waiting for him to react differently. To acknowledge I'm not as pretty as Lauren. He must be disappointed. When I slope my gaze up to level with him, his eyes shine back at me. They are kind, sparkling with a mischievous glint.

He opens his mouth to speak.

This is it.

Maybe he won't say I'm not pretty directly. It's usually a passive-aggressive comment like asking if one of us is adopted. I know it's coming. With his free hand, he points to the taco sack. "I brought tacos, but we need to hurry and eat because they might be getting cold."

Tacos is always a magic word to make my door open.

I invite him in with a hand gesture toward my desk chair. I mean, I'm not going to turn down free tacos. I'll see how this goes. "So, what a mix-up, huh?" I say as I take a seat on the edge of my bed.

His smile is content. He emits a gentle laugh that's full of warmth, and it slowly starts to win me over. "It's pretty funny. Even though I made a massive fool out of myself, now I'm so glad I ran into Lauren because I was super sad I missed out on meeting you."

He sounds so sincere; his words whoosh shivers right to my gut. "I'm sorry about not texting you—"

"Don't," he cuts me off again. After a deep swallow marked by a bob of his Adam's apple, he says, "I don't tell people this, but I know exactly how you feel. It's sort of funny, actually."

"You do?" I give him an angled stare. He can't possibly know how I'm feeling. There's nothing displeasing about his appearance at all. He's extremely handsome. No woman would ever be disappointed to see him.

"Yeah," he goes on. "So, please don't think I'm bragging. I'm only telling you this because I know you'll understand. My sister is a famous pop star." He gestures forward, and tacks on, "Sophie Summers."

"Sophie is your sister!" I slide to the edge of my bed, as there's no way. I don't know her, but this little town of

Mapleton is very proud to have the celebrity call this place home, and everyone knows of her.

"Yeah." His lips straighten into a line of forlornity I recognize as one I use when I talk about my sister. "She's been famous since she was like fourteen. You can imagine the disappointment I get when people ask me what I do. I say, 'I live with my parents and go to college.' I didn't have a job until this week, and it's not even that cool of a job. It pays minimum wage. Trust me, I get what you were feeling. I couldn't be happier that we also have that in common."

My heart stills. No longer sinking as it absorbs everything. I had no idea *Sophie Summers* was his sister. That's crazy. Yeah, she would be impossible to live up to. I swallow down my anxiety, and say, "I thought it was cool you drove a Zamboni."

"Something else we have in common." His smile grows, and my stomach knots relax. He reaches into his bag, pulls out a taco, and hands it to me. Our fingers brush together as I take it, and a spark shoots up my arm like something I've never felt. We both pause, and one of his brows arches above the other while his gaze lingers on me.

I set my taco in my lap and slowly unwrap it. There is never a time I don't enjoy a taco, but my senses are so heightened, this has to be the most delicious taco I've ever smelled. "This looks wonderful."

"They always are." He unwraps one of his tacos and takes a bite. After he chews for a moment, he sets it back on the foil wrapper on my desk and says, "I'm Sam, by the way. Sam Summers. Sorry, I didn't say that sooner, but again, I'm sort of protective about my last name because of Sophie."

A little giggle bleeps out of my lips, like it caught hold of his secret. I can totally understand why he didn't share his name. It's no fun living in your older sibling's shadow. "So," I say as I position my taco for another bite, making sure all the chicken is tucked inside the tortilla. "You already know I think tacos are a perfect first date."

We seem to naturally lean toward each other, drawn in by some invisible force. His body language is open and inviting. Every time I smile, he smiles wider. "So, I'm not going to ask about your sister, because I already know you're sick of talking about her. Tell me, in a perfect world, what's your biggest dream?"

"That's pretty deep." Nobody ever really asked me that. His gaze is steady, and I risk vulnerability. "Is it bad that I don't really have a big one? I mean, I want to be happy, but beyond that, I'm sort of just living."

"I understand that completely." His sentence is punctuated with a heavy sigh that draws me even closer to him. I've never met someone before who I felt instantly got me.

I reach for my water bottle and take a sip, finding it easy to swallow. All night I had this tightness in my throat for not texting him. Now I feel even more terrible when I think about him finding out I wasn't who he thought I was. With a sudden bravery, I hold my voice steady and ask, "Are you disappointed I don't look like Lauren?"

His eyes widen, his eyebrows arching in what I assume is shock. The reaction doesn't last long, as they quickly even into a gentler expression, and his gaze bounces around my face, as if he's taking in every detail. His eyes sparkle even more the longer he looks at me. I hold my breath until he finally speaks, "Not at all. She's pretty. I don't want to feel like I'm giving you a line. Everything always feels so cheesy, but when I first saw you, I just knew your beauty was real." His gaze sweeps to the side for a moment before he says, "Not sure if that even makes any sense..."

My heart instantly flutters in full throttle. I prefer that he didn't deny he thought Lauren is pretty. Now I know he's being truthful, and that makes his compliment to me more potent. I pinch back a smile. It's just one more thing we have in common. We think so much the same. "You didn't ask, but for what it's worth, I'm pretty happy you're you too."

"You know," he starts and then stops while his gaze drops down to his taco. "I thought a perfect meeting with you would be tacos, but that was wrong. I actually think this is so perfect we don't even need tacos."

My smile grows even wider as I stare back at him, his eyes glittering. I know exactly what he means. It's just one more thing we have in common.

Nine

SAM

Two weeks into my job, I'm back at the arena for another home game, which we sadly lost. Now I squeegee water from the heated storage room floor over to the drain, reflecting on what a weird month this is. I started it off as a college student, fully content spending all my free time on the couch. Now, I've got a job, and I'm picking up extra shifts at the arena, learning to do all kinds of things, and the most shocking thing—I have a crush.

We've been texting constantly, and she doesn't talk about any other guys she's dating. It's way too soon to think about exclusivity, but at this point, I would feel nauseous if she were talking to other guys. It's hard to explain, as it's not jealousy. I just know in my gut she's meant to be mine.

Footfalls pull my attention to the door before Cleo peeps his head in. "Are you all done for the night?"

"Yeah, I was just cleaning the floor up."

His dark brows dip lower as he takes a long step in while looking around. "Did you spill something?"

"No." My voice is even as I continue to push the squeegee forward.

"Did I ask you to do that?" Cleo's question is braided with a healthy dose of confusion.

"No." I'm smiling now as I'm shocked. When I had imagined getting a job, I thought I'd be the one staring at the clock, counting down seconds until the time was up, and then bolting out of the door.

That's not the case at all.

I like it here. I found out I like working with my hands. I also enjoy feeling like I accomplished something for the day. "You didn't ask, but I'm happy to help out." I slope my gaze at him. "Unless you would rather I not, but I'm almost finished."

"No, I always appreciate when employees step up." He stuffs his hands in his pockets and does a sweeping scan of the storage room.

"Hey, Cleo, I was going to ask you something." I straighten the handle on my brush and lean on it as if it's my new walking cane.

"What's up?" His eyes latch back on mine. I take a second to assess them, hoping it's not a bad time to bring something up. He looks relatively fine.

"There's, ah." I lean too far on my handle as I've momentarily forgotten I'm holding it up, and not the other way around. The handle tips to the side, taking me with it. I scrabble to catch it midair before it hits the floor. I lean over, grab the handle, and I hurry to stand straight with my attention on Cleo.

He busts out a chuckle and pulls his hands out of his pockets while taking a step closer. "Easy there. If you break the brush, it comes out of your paycheck."

He's fully joking around, and I appreciate his humor. All of the sudden it is super-hot. Swiping my forehead, I steal my gaze back to him. "Ah, there's this girl. Ah—" I pause to take a breath, but he cuts me off.

"She wants a ride on the Zamboni. Doesn't she?"

"How'd you know?"

"They always do." He shakes his head as his gaze floats back to my machine. "It's a serious girl magnet."

"Apparently." I chuckle, glad he understands my predicament. I wasn't trying to attract any women, but the one I found is very sweet. I just want to make her happy. "Is that allowed?"

"Yeah, we offer rides, but she needs to sign a waiver. They are in the main office. The receptionist can grab one for her. That goes for any of your family members too. Family usually thinks it's fun to try it out."

"Well, Sophie hasn't said anything, and Axl can get his own ride."

"So, back to this lady friend, is she your girlfriend?" He gives me a nonchalant side-eye. One that says he doesn't care either way and more or less is making conversation.

"Not yet." I can't help but break into a full smile.

Okay, call me a nerd.

She's completely rearranged my brain.

She's all I thought about today. I can't just say no, even though it's the truth. I'm making my intentions known to everyone, even Cleo. "I want to ask her, but I'm worried it's a little soon. We just met last week."

He pushes his bottom lip out into a thinking position before nodding his head. "If the attraction is there, and you get along well, that's probably good. You don't want some other dude sneaking in there."

"That's exactly what I thought." I rush out a breath of relief as I'm glad he agrees.

"If she needs more time, she'll tell you." He throws up a hand in a casual gesture before tacking on, "It never hurts to ask."

My heart fills up with so much hope. Hearing someone else say it's a good idea seeds my confidence. "Cool." I downplay my excitement and nod at my brush. "I'll finish up here and then grab a form for her."

"Lock up on your way out." He pivots and strides back to the door. I wait until he's all the way down the hall and out of sight before I let my smile crack wide open. I whip out my phone to text.

Me: I'm finishing up at work, but I have a test tomorrow. Is there any way you'd want to meet up to study together at the library?

It only takes a moment, and I get a text back.

Finley: Sure.

It's one word.

I read it over and over. My heart flutters in my chest.

I can't wait to see her.

With my book under my arm, my other hand clenches my phone as I pace outside the library. Every few steps, my gaze drops to my phone.

I check the time, still hasn't moved.

No new texts.

My heart pounds in my chest. Not sure if I'm more nervous tonight than I was last time I saw her. Footfalls behind me alert my attention, and I spin on my heel and see her.

She winks at me.

Like an actual wink.

Who winks?

Apparently, she does.

It's slow and intentional, and it sends a zing right through my chest, taking the long way through my belly, looping some of my intestines into heart-shaped knots before it fizzles out into a landing so super close to my heart, the heat left over from that zingy wink starts to chip away, melting my heart.

Seriously.

Not even exaggerating a little.

Her winks are lethal.

I could wink back. I've never been much of a winker. I might look like my eye is stuck. Instead, I nod, sticking my chin out and practicing my deep voice, "Heeey."

"Hey, Sam." Her gaze looks me up and down.

I shiver, unrelated to her looking-at-me shiver. It's purely from the cold. That's what I try to tell myself, even though I know it's a big giant lie. "Should we go in?" I rotate enough so I angle toward the library and jerk my thumb toward the entrance.

She steps forward, aligning her steps with mine. I reach the door first and open it for her because I'm a perfect gentleman. As she passes through the door, I ponder when exactly it was that I became this perfect gentleman.

Hmm?

Her presence makes me want to stand taller and do all the things that make her feel special.

I've never had this feeling before. We stand near the entrance, surveying the stacks in the back and the rows of tables up front near the librarian. In hindsight, maybe the library wasn't the best place to meet up? I hadn't thought about the fact we must be quiet, and there's a lot of people around. However, I'm in this all the way, and I whisper, "How about we take that table in the back?"

She smiles, and we plod forward until we get to the last table near the back window and drop our books. I plop down on a wooden chair, and she takes the one opposite of me, immediately opening the book she brought.

"What are you studying?" I ask in a quiet voice as I ready my book to look over the chapter review questions.

"Psychology." She raises a shoulder in a lazy shrug. "It's okay if you read the chapter. Then the tests aren't too hard."

"Do you have Professor Lines?" I've heard his name tossed around campus a lot, and know he teaches a lot of the freshman classes.

"Yeah, he's pretty easy." Her attention is on my book. "What are you studying?"

"Intro to Business." I sound as bored of the subject as I am. "Business is obviously my major. I'm not sure what kind of business yet, but it's an okay class."

"Business is a great major." She lets out a frustrated sigh, then proceeds to whisper as she leans forward, "I still don't know what I'm majoring in. I thought maybe I'd know once I got on campus, but if anything, it's more confusing. I just want a normal life, whatever that major is."

I chuckle, because it's exactly how I feel. "Same." I smile at her, and marvel at how her eyes seem to have an extra special sparkle for me. I'd like to think she saves it for me, but it's hard to know. I invited her here to study, but there's something on my mind. I clear my throat and whisper, "Say, can I ask you something?"

"I think so." Tilting her head as if to angle her ear a bit closer, she runs her hand over her hair, tucking all her hair back behind it.

"You don't have to answer if you don't want to, but how come you've never had a boyfriend?"

Her playful smile titters back to bashful, and her gaze lowers to her notebook. "I can't believe my sister told you that."

"Is it true?"

"Yes." Leveling her gaze with mine, she tacks on, "Does that bother you?"

"No, not at all." I slide to the edge of my seat as my heart ticks up a notch. "I was just making sure you hadn't sworn-off dating, or something like that."

"No, not sworn off dating." She pauses while she tosses a slow look over her shoulder. More than likely to check to see if anyone can hear our conversation. When she's satisfied, she returns her attention to me while her fingers hang on to the edge of her notebook. "To be honest, I haven't really ever been asked." Her cheeks immediately blush while her fingers fidget with the notebook corner, lifting it up and fanning through it until the paper has run out, and starting over again. I stare at her thumb, finding it the most adorable thing. "How come you don't have a girlfriend?" Her words are even quieter than before.

I chuckle, as it's sort of like her response but with a twist. "I guess, I haven't really tried."

"Oh." Her brows bend down, and she pulls her hand back, dropping both hands to her lap.

"I mean, I've had dates and went to all the regular high school dances, but I never had the urge to ask them to be a steady girlfriend. I don't know if that makes sense."

"Maybe it makes sense." The tips of her nostrils flare out, as if she's bringing in more oxygen. It's one more thing I'm finding that makes her fascinating.

"I think I'm ready for a girlfriend though." My statement comes out more like a question. I hold her gaze steady, looking for anything, even the tiniest twitch to give me any clues to how she's really feeling. Another little nose flare will be perfect.

"Are you hinting at something?" Her smile grows playful, sending another one of those zinging wooshes to my gut.

"Maybe." I hang on to the first syllable, speaking extra slowly. I don't want to risk saying anything I'll regret, as I'm already completely out of my comfort zone, but I have to know what she's thinking. "Are you in a place right now where you want a boyfriend or are you happy hanging out?"

"I definitely don't want just any boyfriend." She sits up straighter, perfecting her posture. "But, if you're asking what I think you're asking, I can see us spending more time together."

"You can?"

A genuine smile blooms on her lips. "I can, and I'd like it a lot."

The zinging zapping things are getting stronger. This one shoots through my chest and seems to reverberate in my toes so hard, I have to curl them. She's stunning. We have so many things in common. I can't wait to see what else we find out about each other. We haven't even finished this little date yet, but I can't wait to secure the next one. "So, ah, there's this thing tomorrow in the Mapleton City Park."

Her body stills as she waits for me to finish. I pause an extra beat, just so I can stare at her. She's so beautiful. "It's a concert that Bill Baker, the Granite Ice team owner, puts on for charity. He roped my sister into performing, among other people. Would you want to go?"

In my peripheral, the librarian is striding over with a direct line toward our table. I already know what she's going to complain about. I attach my gaze up to her, and say, "Sorry. We'll be quiet."

"Thank you." The librarian's gaze bounces to Finley for a second before she turns on her heel and heads away.

Finley pinches back a smile as her thumb finds the edge of her notebook again, and she's back to fidgeting. "We have to be quiet," she whispers.

"Okay," I mouth, vowing to be quiet, but my stomach growls loudly. It's like a bomb in the silence. I glide my gaze to the side, finding the librarian glaring at me with her readers on the tip of her nose. So, I grab my pencil, reach across the table, and scribble on Finley's notebook: Date tomorrow?

She nods a yes. I want to talk to her more, and since we got cut off, I write another two words on there: Tacos now?

Her look of shock is a tad disappointing.

Tacos never did anything to her.

She takes her pen, scribbling below my words: Study first. Tacos later. I have to get this summary done.

Mocking annoyance, I drop my hand to my stomach and mouth, "Fine."

She jots something else. When she's done, she holds up the notebook for me: Give me fifteen minutes.

I reach across the table, snatch the notebook from her, and write as I roll my bottom lip under. I'm not trying to play games. Just flirt a little. Then I flash what I wrote at her: I feel like I could wait a lifetime for you.

The eye roll is uncalled for, but she smiles in a way that creases her cheeks so much a little dimple pops in the center of her lower cheek. I've never seen that dimple before. It's like she was saving it for the perfect moment. Now I'm obsessed.

I cut a glance toward the time on my phone. Only fourteen more minutes until tacos. Then I waft my gaze back to her dimple, knowing time will fly with this scenery.

Ten

Finley

Eyeing my Crocs, I suck back a big breath.

It's going to be cold standing outside at the park.

If I wear my boots, my feet will hurt so badly, I'll have trouble enjoying myself. My gaze skirts back to my little three-drawer dresser, where I store my winter clothes. Maybe I'll wear two pairs of socks and call it good? I quickly cross the room to grab another pair of wool socks when my phone vibrates on my desk.

Lauren: Do you want to go to the nail salon with me? I'll pay for you to get yours done.

If Lauren could only see my nails now. They are unpolished and chewed all the way down. I've never been one to keep up a manicure. The few times I have gotten my nails done was only because Lauren didn't want to go to the salon alone, which I'm assuming is happening now. I quickly type back:

Me: I would but I have a date with Sam. We are going to that charity concert downtown.

Lauren: You do? That's exciting. You've been spending a lot of time with him.

Me: I know. It's a lot of fun. Maybe I owe you a thank you, but we have a lot in common.

I should invite her because Lauren tends to be the co-dependent type. She has issues being alone. Normally, she has a boyfriend who does everything with her. Now I'm wondering how her date went. I never talked to her about him, but I'm guessing not so well if she's asking me to hang out again.

Me: Hey, how did your hockey guy date go?

Lauren: Hard to say. I think he's amazing, but the vibe was off.

Bunching my lips into a thinking position, I ponder how it's rare Lauren doesn't vibe with someone. She gets along with everyone. It might have been the awkwardness of having Sam crash her date. As much as it's working out for me, I feel terrible that it may have ruined her chance to get to know her date. I wish I could make it up to her somehow...

Me: You should come down to the park. I'm sure he'll be at this concert. It's a team charity thing. There will be lots of people you know, and maybe you can run into him.

My phone double vibrates as I receive a text from both Lauren and Sam.

Lauren: Maybe I'll come down. I'll see if Mom and Dad want to go. I'm not going to call Elijah. He's fine. I just get the vibe he's hung up on his ex.

Me: Got ya.

Sam: I'm just pulling up to your dorm.

Oh, no! I still have to finish getting ready. I drop my phone in my purse, so that it's ready. Grabbing my socks in one hand, and my shoes in the other, I plop down on the edge of my bed to put them on. Inhaling a deep breath, I force my stomach loops to smooth out. This feels so much more like an actual date than the other times I've seen Sam. Everything else was casual. This is us being out in public together. People will see us. He might even introduce me to his sister, or the rest of his family.

This feels like a couple's event.

It seems like a big step.

I'm so excited, I don't need to force a sense of urgency because I'm automatically rushing, and I grab my keys to lock up right as there's a knock on the door.

"Yeah, I'm coming." I rush over, then pause in front of the door. He doesn't need to see me flustered. I take another deep breath, smooth out my sweater, and open the door. "Hi," I say.

He's standing with one hand in his jacket pocket and the other one is holding a single pink rose. Heat flushes across my cheeks, and I smile as he presents my gift. "It's not chili seasoned, but I'm hoping it will do."

"I love it." Biting back a nervous giggle, I take it from him. The petals are tight, hinting they are about to open soon. It's wrapped in beautiful pink tissue paper with one of those water tubes on the stem. I eye the water tube. Even though it's still half full, I decide not to risk it. "Let me put this in water quick." I pivot and walk to my little sink and grab a glass as that's the only thing I have. While I wait for the glass to fill with water, I lift the rose to my nose, but I keep my gaze on Sam.

It's weird how I got used to seeing him already. Like, literally two weeks ago, I didn't even know him. Now it feels like we've known each other much longer. I add the flower to the glass and set it on my desk, so it will be the first thing I see when I come home. Then I cross the room again and grab my heavy coat off the hook. "Are you nervous?" I ask as we walk out together, and I pull the door closed behind me, taking a minute to lock up.

"No." He has on an easy expression. "I'm excited. Are you nervous?"

"I was." I love how honest I can be with him. "It's better now that I see you."

"That's a good thing, right?" It's one of those questions that doesn't need an answer, and he doesn't wait for one either. Instead, he holds his hand out and flashes a flirty smile, the one where the corners of his lips lift into a playful arc, and his perfect teeth peek through.

Nothing feels out of place about holding his hand. It's a natural instinct, and my hand fits perfectly in his larger hand, which sends a sense of protection and comfort back through me. As we walk forward, he gives my hand a gentle squeeze of reassurance and it feels like we're being connected in our own little world. Someplace where we are just building and discovering on our own, and I can't wait to see what it all brings.

Almost every person in town has bundled up in hats and scarves and squeezed into the little Mapleton town square park. I love it when this happens. It brings so much community to everyone as they bustle around.

I can't help but turn my head in all directions. The park is transformed into a fall wonderland, with warm golden lights strung through the trees and leaves crunching underfoot. So far, so good with the Crocs situation. I'm not overly cold, and Sam is right by my side, holding my hand. He brings an aura of warmth that I'm fast becoming addicted to.

A stage is set up at one end of the park, with colorful lights shining on the empty stage. Food trucks line the perimeter of the park, their neon lights advertising specials and delicious scents wafting through the crisp air.

People gather on blankets and lawn chairs. Some snuggle under cozy blankets, while others wrap their hands around hot cups of cocoa or cider. My eyes hover on those people the longest, as I find myself wondering what it will feel like to snuggle under a blanket with Sam.

He looks back at me, as if reading my mind and says, "I didn't even think to bring chairs or anything to sit on." His eyes are wide as if waiting for me to express disappointment.

"It's fine." I gesture forward, brushing his comment away. "I prefer to stand anyway." It's not really the whole truth. I would love to sit in a big cushy lawn chair, but I don't even want to give him the smallest hint I'm anything but excited to be here.

SQUEEEEEEEEEE.

A high-pitched sound pulls my gaze to the stage. Some guy in a Granite Ice warm-up suit and beanie is standing in front of the microphone, and apparently, it's the mic that's making that sound.

Wincing I look back at Sam, who's placed his hands over his ears. "That's Bill Baker, Granite Ice team owner."

"Testing 1, 2, SQUEEEEEEEEEE." More sounds from the stage. Bill's bushy eyebrows furrow with annoyance as he glares at the microphone.

"That is one squeaky mic," I say. Without a conscious effort to do so, my jaw locks into a wince.

Bill let's out a frustrated sigh that the microphone picks up perfectly, clueing us in that it's now, maybe working. He leans forward again, speaking cautiously, "Good evening. Is this finally working?" Bill taps the mic that's still attached to the stand, and it miraculously doesn't squeak. I'm still holding my face in a wince as he goes on, "Thank you all for coming out to support this year's Granite Ice team charity concert. As you may already know, each year we pick a different charity to support. This year, we're donating all the proceeds from the concert and food sales to the Mapleton Fire Department, so eat as much as you can, and enjoy the music."

A soft ripple goes through the crowd, and I grin at Sam. The string of lights above his head cast a bit of a glowing halo on his head. It was oddly fitting, like he was being singled out amongst the crowd as someone who is special. My top teeth dig into my bottom lip as Sam focuses on the stage. His sister has taken her spot and started to play an upbeat song. I don't pretend I listen to pop music, but I definitely know who she is. As much as he says he doesn't like to live in her shadow, there's evidence he's proud of her.

The crowd moves toward the stage, and people dance and sing. I stuff my hands in my pockets and sway along. Sam must have caught me swaying, because he promptly shouts over the music, "Did you want to dance?"

Oh no!

I hate dancing.

Like, come on, I'm wearing Crocs, it's cold, and it takes a lot of work to sway around like that. I'd much rather taco, but Sam's looking back at me, his gorgeous eyes flickering from that golden halo. There's no way I can disappoint him. This is his sister's concert. I'd be a total jerk to say no. "Of course," I shout back, and step closer to him. We stroll out to the dance area. Even though it's a fast song, he takes a step, edging into my space. My heart ramps up so many notches I'm suddenly doing high-intensity cardio as we sway to the beats.

I don't have any moves.

I mean, not unless you count the jiggles.

Sam's gaze never leaves my face, and his smile is wide. He's fully enjoying this moment, so I slap on a matching smile and flail my arms around. I might look like I need medical attention with these moves. Actually, I could call them the "ambulance call." I don't have narrow hips like all the other girls. My hips don't shake, and if I lift my feet, they'll more than likely quake.

Ha. I didn't mean to rhyme. I'm just trying to get through this awkwardness.

He reaches for my hands, squeezing them as he moves them. Maybe that's the sign to stop my ambulance call?

Am I that bad?

After a few beats, he drops my hands again, and I take a hint and leave my arms down close to my body. He takes another step closer, and now I can smell his deodorant or something wafting off him. It's a warm cedar glow that perfectly matches that halo, and I could literally drink it in.

It sends a whoosh of all the feels to my gut. I chuckle a fast, fluttery bleep from all the nerves. The way he has his gaze dialed into mine makes me melt. That song is over, and I am slow to stop. He's still swaying, and I ask, "Did you want to keep dancing?"

"Yeah." That's all he says but his tone clearly informs me he loves this dance thing. He keeps moving, and at this point my stomach erupts into a rumble. Great, now I'm hungry.

The beat changes, slowing down, and he pulls me even closer, hugging me tight, which should be romantic and all, but my side hurts from all that shaking. I'm also embarrassed by how heavy I'm breathing.

I'm wheezing like a Hoover.

This is not how I planned to impress him.

"Are you having a good time?" His lashes lower as he's quite a bit taller than me. Standing this close to him makes me arch my neck all the way back to get a direct look at him.

"Yeah." I fake a sigh, hoping to cover my heavy breathing. I just hate dancing. I'm too self-conscious to enjoy this. He's so sweet with the way he gently guides our steps, and I couldn't ever say anything. "Are you having a good time?"

"The best," he hums as he turns his attention to the sky, gazing out.

"I love this song." It takes all my excess breath to semi-shout over the music. It's a slow song, and we are awfully close, but I still don't think he can hear me. He nods and stares forward.

I focus on how amazing it feels to be in his arms, even if it means I have to strain my brain to make sure I don't stomp all over his feet.

Next to us, I see people ordering food from the nearby truck, and my stomach actually pains. Tossing a casual look over my shoulder, I sneak a glance at the specials. Taco in a bag. The amount of chili seasoning wafting from that truck is unholy. I bite back a groan as my lips pucker from the saliva pooling in the center of my mouth.

Grrrrumble.

Oh, my stomach is not good at playing it cool.

Sam leans back, tilting his head to better see my face. "Are you hungry?"

There is no way I can deny it, as my stomach rumbles again. "A little."

"Why didn't you say something?" He pauses mid-step, dropping his hands from my back and I let out a breath of relief that the dancing is finally over.

"Well, I was just enjoying the moment."

"Let's get in line for something." He points to the truck I had been eyeing, and we both walk at top speed toward it. It takes a fair amount of restraint from me not to bust out into a full smile as I nonchalantly order only one taco in a bag.

We grab our food and a couple of drinks, and Sam leads the way through the crowded outskirts where we attempt to find a place to eat. The tables are mostly taken, and the ground looks too cold to sit on. "How about we sit on that bench?" He gestures across the park, near the little pond.

"That works." I start walking, not waiting to pick at my food. I grab my fork and scoop up a nice meaty chunk and stuff it in my mouth as we walk. "This is sooo good."

He follows my lead, taking a bite of his food too and hums through his chewing. "So good."

There's an extra shake, or ten, of salt in this taco meat, but I don't even care. It's heaven, especially after working up an appetite dancing. We make it to the bench, and no sooner do we sit down, when a blackbird lands at our feet. I'm about to comment on how cute he is, but he flaps his wings enough to look as if he's coming right toward Sam's taco. "Get!" He waves the bird off. His attempt is in vain, and soon five of his blackbird friends have joined him. We have a whole flock pecking near our feet. The birds are much bigger than I've ever noticed a blackbird to be, and they make me quite anxious.

"Ah, should we go back up?"

"Get out of here!" He flicks his hand out, attempting to wave them off, but they are not fazed. If anything, they crowd in more, and I hate this worse than the dancing.

"Should I give them my taco?" I can't believe I'd ever mutter such foolishness, but they are flapping their wings, crowding us in, and my heart raises a beat.

"Aw." He stands, but the birds take that as an invitation, and one flies up and goes right for his bag. Startling, he jerks his shoulders up as he drops his bag, calling to me, "Let's just get out of here."

He doesn't have to tell me twice. I drop my bag too, hoping that will deter them from following us, and I speedwalk back the way we came. We are quiet as we walk, and then we inch back so close to the dance area, my heart just sinks.

More dying.

I mean dancing.

I recognize the twinkle in his eye as the corner of his lips tip up slowly, "Did you want to dance again?"

I fake a smile, but my heart can't fake what my face can, and I leak out a groan so strong it sounds like something is dying inside my throat.

"Are you okay?" His concern is instant, staring at me with unmasked horror.

"I'm fine," I rush to cover my blunder. "I'll dance if you really want to, but I'm also fine just standing here."

"I'll dance if you want," his reply is instant, but I freeze, locking my gaze on him.

He's cute.

Not just a little attractive, but so dreamy with those plush lips and chiseled cheekbones. I want him to like me, like really like me, but if he's one of those guys who wants a girl who goes out clubbing and dancing all the time, that's just not me.

Maybe I should have taken the hint since his sister is a music professional, but it hadn't dawned on me.

I stare back at him, bouncing my gaze from the halo—it's back and gleaming stronger than ever—to his eyes and lips. Maybe I was kidding myself by thinking this would be fun.

Add to it, the temperature dropped, and my feet are freezing. I want to stay here to be with him, but I really don't want to stay here. If that makes any sense.

He slowly holds his hand out, a romantic gesture meant to lead me out to the dance floor. As much as I crave being near him, my body revolts, and I cringe.

Then I blink.

And I stare a tad longer.

"Uh, can I be honest with you?" I shiver from the cold right as I ask, confirming I'm attempting the right thing.

He tips his head closer, looking at me with a pensive expression and a deep crease in the center of his forehead. "Always."

I trap my bottom lip, weighing the risk one final time. I don't want to offend him. He planned this date, and he's been so thoughtful, but I feel the strong need to be straightforward. "I love that you planned this date, because it's your sister's concert and all. I can see how proud you are, and how much fun you're having. I hate to be a downer, but I'm freezing, hungry, and I really hate dancing. I'm so sorry, but maybe I should just go home, and then you can enjoy your night out."

I hold my breath, waiting for his expression to sour. Instead, he jabs a finger toward me in agreement. "I hate it too."

"Y-you do?" I stammer as I rewind my brain for clues as he looks so content and even happy.

"Yes, I hate it. I'm not a fan of this music. I know it's my sister, but I hear it all the time," he grouses. "I'm cold and I'm actually really upset I lost my taco."

I'm the first one to leak out a joyless chuckle. I can't help but ask, "Why didn't you say something?"

"I thought you were enjoying it." He blows out a breath I can only describe as cleansing. "We can leave right now."

It's a miracle.

We agree on one more thing. My heart instantly fills so full, it flutters as it pumps. "Where do you want to go?" I ask as I look around. Most of the town seems to be in the park. I doubt anything else is going on tonight. As much as I hate it here, I'm not ready for our date to be over.

A smile tugs on his lips, and he holds his hand out for me to grab. This time I take it, and it tugs me toward him until I'm right on his side.

"How about tacos some place warm?" He squints at me, two adorable lines crease in the corners of his eyes.

I can't reply fast enough, "Yes. Yes. A thousand times." Our steps can't sync fast enough as we beeline toward the exit gate, neither of us asking where we're going from here. Ted's Tacos is just around the corner, and they always have a perfect corner booth. I'm feeling at ease now that we've been able to be honest with each other, but there's a niggling in the back of my head encouraging me to confess one more thing, "Say, since we're being honest with each other," I start, giving him a warning side-eye.

"Yeah." His voice seems to weaken as his steps come to a halt, and he turns toward me, his eyes pacing over my face. "Is something wrong?"

"Not at all." I wag my head back and forth. "It's something silly that's been bothering me. Maybe I'm an overly honest person, but I thought you should know, that night when we were first texting—" I cut myself off to take a breath and continue, "That really wasn't me. I didn't want to text you. I'm not really the kind of girl who does that sort of thing. My sister was doing all that. I was actually really mad at her. When I saw how sweet you seemed, I decided it was okay." I tug one side of my lips into an anticlimactic smile. "So, nothing huge. Just wanted to be honest."

"Thank you for sharing." His expression remains neutral. "You're right. It's not a big deal to me at all. I'm glad you felt comfortable telling me that. And it's actually a little adorable."

"How so?" I chew my lips, unsure of where this is going. Like adorable has a spectrum. Puppies are adorable. It's the kind of description you use to express fondness, but it felt lacking, like something you'd say to a little sister.

"How are you adorable?" he echoes, with a knowing smirk. "It means, I enjoy spending time with you, and it's hard to describe."

I wait, staring at his lips for another word. Something that tells me he might possibly like me differently than a little sister. I know it's early to express such things, but my heart crawls in my throat as a new sensation wars inside me. I don't really want to be adorable. I mean, I'm glad I'm not ugly. I run my hand through my hair and stare back at him, wondering what it feels like to be more than adorable.

As if he's reading that my mind needs further consolation, he drops his hand to my hip, sending a whoosh to my gut. "Finley, you know I like you, right?"

No argument here! I flatten my palm to my chest, as now it's having a hard time moving. "Aw, I wasn't sure."

His eyes hang on mine, wide and sparkling. It's like we both know it's too soon to say anything more because it is still so soon to say it. We both feel it. One corner of his lips pulls up, and his focus drops to my mouth, causing my cheeks to blush. I've never kissed anyone.

Never wanted to.

Until now.

I lean forward a little, hoping he gets the hint. His lips part, and mine tingle with yearning...

Thud. Thud. Thud.

I startle from a slow rhythmic thud, echoing off the pavement. Our gazes break off each other and pull to the side as an elderly woman almost sideswipes us with her walker as she moves to step around us. A faint scent of talcum powder and lavender wafts under my nose when she plants her gaze on us, and her tone is spry, "Pardon me for needing to use the sidewalk."

"Sorry." I wince as my gaze follows her on with her stroll. My shoulders droop as I return my gaze to Sam, a crestfallen expression has taken over his face. He quickly recovers a smile when he catches my gaze and nods toward Ted's.

"Shall we taco on?" he says, and we move together, taking each other's hand.

Some people might be concerned they'd be getting into a bit of a rut too soon, but for me, this is exactly what I prefer.

Predictability.

Companionship.

And all the tacos I can dream of...

Now, if we can just complete that kiss next time, then we're perfect.

Eleven

SAM

It's Fanboni Night. One of the games reserved for fan rides on the Zamboni between periods. It couldn't have come with better timing. The Mapleton arena is blanketed with navy and orange. Most of the seats are packed with fans, some holding handmade signs. We just finished the first period, and the scoreboard hangs above, showing we are already behind by one.

It's been a tough season.

We aren't without hope.

My Zamboni hums forward, and I feel the smoothness of the ice as I take a lap around to wave at the fans, and it's now my reflex to look for Finley's face.

It's getting harder and harder to spend time away from Finley. Sure, we text when we aren't together, but I find myself consumed by thoughts of her when she's not around. It makes it harder for me to do basic things.

Like eating tacos.

Every time I eat one, I think about how much she also loves them.

Or walking to class. I think about how much I would enjoy walking next to her, or I wonder if she's walking and maybe her feet are chilly like mine.

It makes sense for us to be together. We have so much in common, and if everything goes well tonight, I'm going to tell her how I'm feeling.

I made sure she knew to meet me down by the ice for the first ride. The announcer gives instructions to the riders who signed up for a lap. I secretly hold my breath and wish there's no one but Finley.

Because at least for me, there is no one but her.

My heart knows it as much as my brain. It's crazy too soon, but crazy seems to be our theme.

She's where I asked her to be. In front of the fan line, standing in her puffy coat with her hands in pink mittens. My eyes draw to hers, as if we're held together by some invisible force. We both pinch back secret smiles as the attendant gives her the clearance to walk onto the ice.

My heart slams against my chest. This moment is huge for us. It's full circle. It's the request that brought us together.

This Zamboni has an extra seat that's perfect for passengers. I can't help but daydream that it didn't. It would be even cooler if I could hold her in my lap, but I quickly let go of that fantasy. I reach my hand down to her and help her up the steps and smile at her. No words are needed because our hands are locked together. It's much more than a casual hello. This is our fingertips brushing over each other's on purpose, because they burn to be this close to her. This is me stealing an inhalation of her perfect scent and holding it in as long as I can before I exhale. It's me using all my control not to stare at those perfect pouty lips, because I can't stop thinking about what it will be like to kiss her.

Before I lose my mind, I steal my gaze back to the ice and do what the crowd expects, steering the machine around for a single lap. "What do you think, Miss Crazy?" I ask her as soon as we are in motion. "Pretty surreal that this is happening?"

It's a question with two meanings.

The first, of course, is the reference to me finally giving her the ride she asked for, but the latter of the meanings secretly refers to how unreal it is that I'm so quickly falling for her. From the way she looks at me, I know she is falling too. Every time I glance at her, I seem to be witnessing her falling a little more. Her gaze grows more dreamlike, and her smile grows wistful. She's so incredibly stunning.

The crowd rumbles around us, cheering us on, but it's just the two of us in my world. "I can't believe it's happening, either," she coos, and I detect a double meaning too. Unfortunately, our lap is over too soon, and there's a long line of fans waiting for a turn. I pull to a stop by the edge of the ice and take her hand to help her down from her seat. "Wait for me after the game?" I squeeze her hand, not hard. More like I'm transferring all my adoration to her.

"Of course." She offers a committal nod, all hints of previous bashfulness completely dissipated. Then she steps down from my machine. I stare after her, longingly. I can't wait much longer to tell her my feelings. It's getting harder and harder to hold it in.

Everything feels so perfect.

After the game, I lock up the storage room and stuff my hands in my coat pockets as I walk back through the tunnels to the lobby. Finley's standing right where we agreed to meet, with her back lazily against the wall outside the ticket office. "Hey, you," I call out softly, aware of how my throat tightens from the sight of her. My body is fast becoming aware of her nearness, and discomfort erupts in my chest.

"Hey." Her reply is much softer, and she hits me with a smirk that is so hot, if we were standing by the ice, it would melt it all. I stop in front of her, crossing my arms across my chest. Not because I'm cross. It's quite the opposite. I've got so much fluttering inside of me, I feel as if I must hold my chest steady. "Thanks for the ride again," she says while entwining her gaze into mine. "It was perfect."

"Was it?" I tip my head to the side. I can't help musing how it would have been better had it just been the two of us without any crowd.

"Yeah, why not?" She chuckles, adding, "We didn't crash into anything, and no blackbirds attacked us."

"Right." I reach out, asserting my position by grabbing both of her hands and tugging her closer to me. "That part was perfect, but I sort of felt like it would have been better if we were alone."

"Oh, yeah." Her chin tilts up. "Well, we are alone now."

"That's true." Tossing a glance down the hall, I confirm the lobby is nearly emptied out. The lights have been dimmed. If it wasn't for my janitor's set of keys stuffed in my pocket, I might be nervous that we were locked in. "In that case." I inch my feet a tad closer and touch our toes. I spark a bigger smile when I notice that neither one of us has proper foot attire on. Me in my sandals. Her in Crocs. Our feet look so perfectly happy parked against each other, I'm done. It's an odd thing to take as a sign, but I can't hold my feelings in anymore.

"I know this may seem out of the blue, and even though that ride tonight was short, it was everything. I hope it's just the start of even more." I pause, steal a look at our perfect toes together, and raise my gaze back to level with hers. Vowing not to be awkward or shy, I barrel on with nothing but honesty, "I'm really starting to like you." I stop, but then tack on in a super snappy pace, "Like a lot."

She blinks in slow motion, and I hold my breath as I pray that's not a bad sign.

Man, do I want to kiss her.

She's just pulling me in with the softest gaze.

Don't do it.

I force my gaze to stay on her eyes because if I dare move even a tad south, I'm going to lean in.

I can't risk it.

Not until I hear her reply, and she's stone-cold quiet.

"Finley," I risk after the longest beat of silence has slapped a sheen of sweat on my low back. I don't need a declaration of love. I would like to know if she's at least a little on the same page.

She shifts, squeezing my hands back, and it sends a lightning bolt straight to my heart. "Same."

"Same?" I repeat as I clearly understand the definition of the word, but I said a lot of words, and I'm not sure what exactly she's saming.

"I feel like I'm in a movie, or a dream, and I can't stop thinking about how lucky I am, because I..." she pauses, like she planned that pause just to taunt me. She takes a moment to dig her teeth into her perfect pouty lip, before she adds, "I like you too."

Heaven help me. My heart just backflipped.

"How much?" I blurt it out, my smirk tips into one filled with confidence. It's crazy how much having the girl I like, like me back, makes me instantly playful.

"What do you mean how much?" Her brow bends down.

Tipping my head closer to hers, I drop my tone and rasp, "Do you like me enough to let me kiss you?"

Blush gushes over the tops of the little freckles that dot her cheeks. She doesn't waver when her inviting smile seems to twist around her single-word answer, "Yes."

There isn't a thing on the planet that could deter me from the task at hand. Her lips fold together in the perfect pout, just waiting for me. I drop her hands and bring one of mine to her waist and the other to her chin.

She's tense.

Maybe scared.

When I stare deeply into her eyes, I see a kaleidoscope of all the memories we are going to make.

I'm completely at ease.

Now my goal is to first make her relax. I tip my chin down, but instead of aiming for her lips, I drop a kiss on her cheek. Her brow quivers, as if she's not sure if she should be con-fused or content. Her eyes stay hooked on me when I move my thumb from her chin to her lips and softly run the length of them. I'm overcome with the feeling I'm living in slow motion. My senses heighten, and I just marvel at her.

Goosebumps dot my spine and her body sags toward me.

I drop a chaste kiss in the perfect middle of her mouth, and I pull back, teasing her by grazing my teeth along her lip. I'm not about taking more than she wants to give, and she still seems nervous.

Her hand slides around my waist, as if to tell me that it's not enough. I duck my head down again, taking my time to connect to her lips in the slowest setting. Her lips lolled into mine as if they were molded for this moment. My heart constricts as if being marked, and I have not one doubt in my head—or heart—this woman is going to drive me crazy in the best of ways.

Epilogue

Flattening my palm against my thigh, I swipe the sweat off on my new leggings.

"Relax." Sam wraps a hand around the small of my back, taking his place next to me as he opens the front door to his house. "It's going to be fun."

I adjust the poinsettia I bought this morning for a hostess gift, holding it in the center of my body. I grasp the plant tightly, grateful to have something to hang on to, while I exhale slowly and glue on a smile.

He's right, even though I'm wishing we would have arranged an earlier meet-the-parents event that wasn't Christmas. This is the first time I've been invited to hang out. My stomach is looping into so many knots, I'm praying I don't embarrass myself...or Sam. Everything has been going so well for us, but part of that might be because we are homebodies who don't really socialize much. "It's hard to relax when I'm awkward in social settings."

"You're not awkward at all." He waves me over the threshold, and the wooden floorboards creak underfoot. Grinning as we pass the faded cream peeling paint on the walls, I find them oddly calming. It's weird when you know you're going to be spending Christmas with an international pop superstar, but seeing their family home look like a regular house with flaws is exactly what I needed. The dated furniture shows patterns of red-and-cream plaid, but everything is clean.

Walking toward the aromas of roasting turkey and rosemary, my stomach never disappoints, promptly churning in happiness. "Smells amazing," I whisper as I take a moment to slip out of my Crocs. I came prepared, knowing I'd have to take off my shoes, and made sure I wore cute socks. Wiggling my toes in my festive green-and-red striped Christmas socks. I love them so much I might be tempted to keep them in the drawer year-round. The problem is there's a lot of snow tracked into the little entryway, and I can't step around it, and I immediately soak my sock with icy water.

"Oh no," I breathe out as the water is so chilly it stings my toes. "My socks are soaked."

"Sorry. That's my fault. I was too excited to slip off my shoes." Sam looks back at his steps, stomping off the remaining snow from his shoes before kicking them aside. "Why don't you take your socks off and throw them over the radiator for a few minutes?"

I hate to take them off, because I especially picked them out to look cute, but I can't walk around with wet socks. I slip them off, and Sam places them on the window ledge above the hissing radiator.

"Sam?" a woman's voice, I assume is his mom, calls from around the corner. Soon she appears in the living room. She's wearing a black dress that is so long it almost touches the floor, and her hair is pinned up. Her gaze quickly shifts to me, and her eyebrows float up as she exclaims, "Oh, Finley!"

I freeze.

My mouth clams up.

My legs stop.

I'm a statue.

She stares at me, waiting for me to reply. When I don't, Sam steps forward. "Yes, this is Finley." He nods back at his mom. "This is my mom, Susan."

"Nice to meet you, Finley." His mom nods at me again.

I still don't work.

I don't know why!

There's nothing strange or shocking about her appearance, and their home is inviting as any other home. "Is everything alright?" His mom's smile begins to deflate as her gaze bounces from Sam to me. Just when I think my words are gone forever, I shove my poinsettia toward her and blurt out, "I have plant."

"You have plant?" she echoes, nodding while her mouth begins to shape into a perfect O. "Oh! You don't speak English." Her gaze cuts back to Sam. "You never told us she was foreign." Then she quickly cuts her gaze back at me. "Hablas Espanol?"

How did I mess this up in the first minute?

"I speak it," I rush out in the most robot voice. "I speak American."

Sam does not help because he's keeling over at the waist, busting out in laughter.

"Are they here?" a boisterous voice I quickly diagnose as Sam's father yells, and he joins us in the living room.

"Yes, Shawn. Sam and Finley are here." Sam's mom turns toward his dad. "Finley doesn't speak English."

"I speak it," I chime in, my cheeks flaming. "I forgot for a moment."

"That's no problem. We can get Siri to translate." Sam's dad turns toward the opposite wall. "Suri, can you translate Spanish into English?"

By this point, Sam has dropped to his knees, holding his side, and he looks as if he's about to drop the rest of the way to the floor.

I'm fending for myself when I assert myself louder, "I speak English."

His mom waves me off. "Oh dear, we understand you have trouble. You do the best you can."

Sighing, I give up. I'll have to try to explain later. I'm still holding the plant, and I take a deep breath and try to present it to her again. "I brought you *a* plant." Making sure to enunciate my correct grammar this time, I stress each syllable.

"Thank you." Sam's mom receives my plant. I can tell by the way her words are extra pronounced, she's not convinced I speak their language. "Come on in." She waves us forward. "I'm going to check on the turkey but make yourself at home." She over enunciates every other word and talks with her hands.

Sam's parents disappear into the kitchen. Sam's laughter dies into a low moan as he straightens up and moves to stand next to me again. I glare at him, and whisper, "Thanks for helping me."

Shaking his head, he whisper-shouts back, "You have to admit it's super funny, especially with all the tacos you eat."

I button my bottom lip tightly, as this is so embarrassing.

Sam wraps an arm around my back, pulling me into his side as he drops his mouth to my ear. "Well, remember how our first date was horrendous, but everything worked out perfectly? Maybe this is a good sign. It can only go up from here."

"I guess," I murmur, trying to see how this could possibly be a good thing.

"Put it this way, if tacos can fall apart but still be amazing, we can totally salvage our night."

Lifting my brows, my whole expression perks up.

Now, he's speaking my language.

I follow Sam to the sofa, feeling a little stiff as I lower myself. "Relax," Sam says again as his hand finds my knee, giving it a little squeeze. "You're doing great."

I stare forward at the lovely Christmas tree, adorned in familiar hues of maroon and gold, with twinkling white lights dotting its evergreen branches. It seems silly, but something so ordinary as the family Christmas tree reminds me again that it's a normal family, and there's nothing scary. It radiates warmth, joy, and family togetherness, foreshadowing all the hours people will spend by this tree. I take deep breaths as I center myself on the tree. For a moment, I'm calm.

The front door whips open, bringing in a gust of cold air, and drawing our attention to Sophie and Axl. They're always adorable. Sophie leads the way wearing a long cream sweaterdress with her dark hair in long waves down her back. Axl shuffles behind her with a stack of presents balanced in his hands, and he shuts the door with a swift kick of his foot. "What's up, guys?" Axl's gaze finds us as he easily makes himself at home, first setting the stack of presents next to the tree, and he hops over the love seat armrest and drops down.

I'm sort of jealous of how comfortable he looks in his in-laws' house, and it helps to put me at ease—a little. He's been a part of this family for a while now. I guess some things just take some getting used to.

"Just hanging out, waiting for you two to show up." Sam's teasing tone is meant to be a dig, but nobody even shows the least bit of offense.

"It took me so much longer to wrap presents than I had planned." Sophie unwinds a cherry-red scarf from around her neck and places it on the coatrack before she gracefully walks over to the love seat to join Axl. Then she plants her gaze on me. "Did my dad tell you any of his famous Mapleton stories yet?"

"No." I shake my head, recalling the few words he said to me. "He didn't, but I accidentally made them think I don't speak English."

"You what?" Sophie's bright-red lips spread into a line of amusement. "How did that happen?"

"I just got nervous and forgot how to talk." I'm quiet as I shift my gaze back to the kitchen, hoping they don't hear. I don't want them to think I'd ever gossip about them or anything. I don't need anything else to make a terrible impression.

"Oh, that's funny." Axl chortles, but it's in good nature, and he quickly recovers by leveling his gaze with mine and saying, "There's no need to be nervous. They are totally cool. Sam's the only other weird one in this family—"

"Ha!" Sam cuts him off with a big sarcastic laugh. "You aren't telling her anything she doesn't already know."

A scuffle by the door pulls my gaze to Sam's mom carrying a tray of little white mugs. She walks it over to the wood coffee table in front of the couch and sets it down. Then she points to it and looks at me. "Hot. Coco."

"Mom." Sam leans forward, taking two cups, giving me one before leaning back with his own cup. "Thank you, but Finley speaks English just fine. Please stop that."

"You do?" One of his mom's eyebrows pins on me in hesitation, and it's then I realize she might be as nervous as I am. She's clearly gone out of her way to make her home so inviting tonight with a beautiful Christmas tree and this dinner. I need to get over my nerves, and it will likely help everyone.

I smile weakly at her, hoping she accepts my confession this time. "I speak English. I was just nervous. Sorry to confuse you."

"Oh, that's ...good." Her eyes swell wide for a moment before they deflate back to a normal width, and she lets out a little giggle as she cuts a glance back at Sam. "I was so confused, you never mentioned the language barrier before, but then I was thinking you did that to play a joke on me." Her giggles pick up into laughs and Sam joins in.

"That would be horribly rude," he says through a chuckle.

"Not for you," Axl cuts in, laughter chugging out from his chest too. "Do you remember the first time I met your parents; you talked me into having a water gun fight in the house."

"That's right." Sam's laughing at full speed again, his mom joining in. The whole room seems to ring with joy. Even though they are laughing about what I did, I don't feel as if they are making fun of me. It's more of just laughing with me.

"What's all the commotion about?" Sam's dad strides in. He's ready for Christmas in a red plaid sweater and dark trousers. He has one of those faces that looks as if he doesn't know how to wear any other expression than a smile, and he leans his back against the doorframe, waiting to join in the fun.

"Finley really does speak English," Sam says to his dad. "It was a mix-up."

His jaw drops slightly, hinting he's holding back a smirk. "Either way, we are happy to have her. I was all set to have Siri help out."

"Right," Sams says, as his chuckles are still coming strong. I'm getting the sense this family enjoys being together.

"Hey, speaking of something funny." His dad's gaze zeros in on me.

"Not the story of the wild monkeys!" Sophie and Sam both shout at the same time.

"I wasn't going to say a word about that." Sam's dad shakes his head, faking innocence. There's a gleam in his eye that tells me otherwise, and he takes a moment to scratch his chin as if he's thinking of something else to say. "Have you ever heard of Mapleton's famous sock stealing squirrel?"

"Ah, what?" I look to Sam to see if he has answers. He's reclined all the way back into the sofa, with one leg crossed over the top of the other one, looking as if he's content to listen to stories all night. I focus back on his dad. "I have not, but it sounds fascinating."

"Let me tell you." He gestures forward with the ease of a natural storyteller. I find myself also leaning back into the sofa as he goes on, "It's not just one squirrel but it's apparently a generation that dates back decades when hanging laundry outside to dry was popular. It always happens when you least expect it, but they have a radar for knowing the moment you set out fresh laundry on the line, and you turn your back for just a second and wham—"

"Dinner's done!" Sam's mom pops her head back in, and I startle. Everyone promptly gets up, following her back to the table.

Sam pulls out a chair, lowering his hand in a gesture toward it. "You can sit here."

I sit and find a napkin next to my plate, and I take a moment to smooth it on my lap. By the time I look up, all the food is already circulating the table.

Sam's dad returns to the story, "You may be thinking, so what about a squirrel that steals socks? That's quite boring, right?" He points to me, waiting for me to reply.

"Right." I say as Sam pushes a giant bowl of mashed potatoes into my hands. Taking it, I scoop out a pile and then pass it along to Sophie. It's like a conveyor belt, and Sam's ready to hand me a platter of turkey. That's even bigger than the potato bowl. With one eye on Sam's dad, I dish myself up.

"You see, that's what everyone says. Who cares that he steals socks. That's actually your fault for leaving them outside, right?" He holds up a finger in pause as he is handed a bowl of salad, and he takes the tongs and dishes himself a huge helping before passing the bowl to his wife. Then he plants his gaze on me and says in a softer tone, "It's all fun and games until you see a squirrel wearing your sock around town on his tail like a tail warmer."

My smile tugs wider. I resist laughing as I'm waiting for everyone else to chuckle first, but nobody laughs. Everyone has a serious line pinned on their lips. "It's true," Sam agrees while Sophie and Axl nod their heads.

"I've lived here most of my life, and I've never seen a squirrel wear a sock," I say slowly as I know they are pulling my leg. It makes for a funny story though, and I appreciate him trying to involve me in the conversation. All the food has circulated and found a spot to rest in the center of the table, and I cut into my turkey, tender and moist. My mouth is watering as I take a giant bite, and hints of butter hit my taste buds first. Butter wasn't what I was expecting, but it's delicious.

"It's true." Sam's mom says in between bites. "I've lost quite a few pairs of socks myself when I was younger. On hot days, I used to take them off to run through the water sprinkler in my parents' backyard. I learned my lesson the hard way."

I chuckle, as I guess it could be possible but not likely. Mapleton is known for having a lot of town legends. I've learned most are just silly tales. Sam's mom focuses on me with a warm smile. "So, you say you're from Mapleton. That must mean your family is here too then."

"Yeah, my parents live over on Applecart Avenue, right in town. My mom's taught at the grade school forever, and my dad drives a truck for the post office." I lift a shoulder in an anti-climactic shrug, as it seems boring compared to having a famous pop singer in your family and a professional hockey player as a son-in-law. "We're a pretty average family."

"Your family sounds lovely—"

Kapow!

I startle; my spine straightens as my gaze slams toward the front of the house, a deafening sound echoing.

Clunk.

Everyone's gazes are now turned toward the front of the house, and Axl and Shawn stand, taking a few steps closer to the front room.

Thud.

That one was the loudest of the series of sounds, and it held in the air like punctuation on a long sentence. We all seem to hold our breath as we wait for another noise. I slowly level my gaze with Sam's and whisper, "What was that?"

"It sounded like the front door slamming. Maybe the wind blew it open?" Shawn says, and now we're all on our feet, inching toward the front. I'm not ashamed to admit I'm hanging out in the back of the pack, but I might be the first one to notice the radiator with only one striped Christmas sock on it. "My sock is gone!" I gasp.

"I'm sure it just fell off." Sam steps forward, peeking behind the radiator. When nothing turns up, he drops to the floor, glancing around. Everything in the entryway is neat, with not one shoe out of place. My socks are bright red and green that contrast to the pale white walls in this room, so they should stick out.

"You guys are pulling my leg." I cross the room and retrieve my lone sock as I scan everywhere to see where the matching one could have gone.

It's nowhere!

Like it was sucked into a void.

"Hey." Sophie's finger juts forward. "Did you leave the window cracked open?"

Above the radiator is a small window. Sure enough, it's cracked open a couple of inches at the bottom. I set my socks there just a few moments ago, and I don't remember noticing it open like that. This is an older farm-style house, and that window is more than likely heavy to pull up. There's no way anything other than a human could slide it open. Now, I know they are playing a joke on me, and I laugh full-heartedly. "You guys almost had me." I shake my head as my gaze bounces from each one of them. I'm now trying to see who has my sock. Such teasers. No one has even so much as a gleam in their eyes. "You guys had me going," I praise, hoping they'll fess up and return my sock. It's one of my favorite pairs. "How'd you set everything up to make all that noise when we were all at the table?"

Every pair of eyes seems to round more, and they are all stone-cold quiet. They are awfully good at keeping secrets. I bet they rehearsed this. "Come on." I sigh. "It's over. It was funny, and you got my heart racing, but I want my sock back now."

"We don't have it." Sophie's face has gone ashen as she stares back at me. "Trust me, this isn't planned. We are as stumped as you are."

"What are you saying?" A chuckle leaks out. I'm about to say the most ridiculous thing ever. "A squirrel stole my sock?"

Shawn shrugs with his face. "I don't know what happened, but we wouldn't hide it from you. That seems cruel. I'm happy to get you a new pair though."

My brows nearly pin together as confusion buds in the front of my brain. This is absurd. I look back to Sam, hoping he'll rescue me with his rascally smile and confess it's all an initiation joke. He's as serious as he's ever been when he shrugs and says, "Maybe he heard you doubt he existed, and he had to come prove his point."

I roll my eyes, and back away from the radiator with my single sock in hand. They are too good at playing, but I know the truth. There's no way a squirrel managed to steal my sock.

After all, that was just a story...

"Hey, come with me," Sam whispers, as he slides in next to me, and grabs my hand. My fingers naturally lace between his. He's already pulling me toward the hallway. "They'll be huge, but I'll grab you a pair of mine."

"Was this a setup?" I'm still scanning along the walls, looking for somewhere he might have moved my sock. This is the most absurd thing.

"No, not at all." I expect him to chuckle, but his expression is serious as he leads me back to his room, and waves me inside. "I have ankle socks that should work for you." His room is plain with only a bed, neatly made. There's a small dresser on the opposite wall, which he heads to right away, opening the top drawer.

"Did you hide all your stuffed animals before I came?" I joke, as I can't find a single decorative item in his room. I think a person's room tells a lot about them, and his room is low-key—a lot like him. What you see is what you get.

"Nah, I used to have a stuffed dragon when I was little, but it's been a while since I've seen him around." He turns around, holding up his other hand with a small box in it.

It's a really small box with *velvet*.

The kind you get in jewelry stores. My heart ramps up as I eye it playfully. "Did you stuff my sock into there?"

"No, it's part of your gift."

"Oh," is all I manage.

"It's just something I saw, and it made me think of you. Since we're opening gifts with my family, I didn't want to give it to you with the rest of your gift because I sort of wanted this moment to just be us. I was going to wait until later after my parents go to bed, but I can't wait anymore."

"Sam," I'm about to say he shouldn't have spent so much money, but he opens the box. Inside is a delicate white gold chain with a decent-sized diamond pendant.

I stare at it, quiet for a second as it's a rather impressive piece of jewelry. "It's beautiful."

"No, you are." I raise my gaze, locking it with his, as it really is my favorite safe place. He's never shy about complimenting me. It's funny after all these weeks of hearing him say that I'm finally starting to believe it. "That's not really all..." He pauses, then starts to speak again, "Phew, did you ever have that moment where your heart is telling you to say something, but your mouth's like, 'don't be an idiot. Just stay shut?'"

Sam always makes me smile, and I let out a laugh. "Sure, I've found that's usually my body's last effort to prevent me from being an idiot."

"Right. I'm hoping I'm not making a mistake, because this feels right." He stops, clears his throat, and a single bead of sweat bubbles on his temples. He's usually the calm one, and this is the most I've ever seen him struggle. "We've been dating for a while." His voice cracks, and he looks to the floor before raising his gaze again. "Honestly, you're easily the best part of every day. Uh, I guess I want to ask—"

"Are you about to propose?" I playfully interject to try to lighten the mood because he looks like he's about to pass out.

His eyes spring wide with alarm. "No! I mean—uh, not that like I would never, but like, maybe, if we make it to that point—not that I'm doubting it, but, man, I'm messing this up."

Chuckling, I grab his hand, pulling it close to my chest as I take a step closer to him, and wrap my free arm around his neck. "Relax," I say, dialing my gaze into his. "It's just me."

"You're right." He blows out a heavy breath and smiles. "Finley, I should have asked you this a while ago, but will you be my girlfriend?"

"Took you long enough." I've never smiled bigger, and I tip my head up even more, readying myself for a kiss. "Only if we can kiss on it?"

An easy grin spreads across his face as he lowers his lips to mine, pressing the sweetest kiss into them. His lips are soft, pulling me to him, and I'm grinning by the time we break away.

We stand in silence for a moment. I'm full of unspoken things, like I can't help but think about how crazy these last several weeks have been. Outside Sam's window, a wintry mix of fluffy snowflakes and wind start to spiral around, and I find myself thinking, I'm the luckiest woman alive. Then another thought pops into my head—at least that squirrel has a nice warm sock...

Oh man, since when do I care about squirrels?

Bonus Epilogue

It has been a year to the day since I first started driving the Zamboni. I could not have guessed my life could be so completely flipped upside down from taking this job. Apparently, I've been on the fast track with my career as I was recently offered an assistant facility manager position. Now I have full-time hours. It's not glamorous work as I do all the snow removal, and a lot of random maintenance, but I'm learning a lot. The pay is actually pretty good, and I was able to move out from my parents' house and get a small one-bedroom apartment near the Mapleton college campus.

Today is also exactly 365 days since I first spoke to Finley. Every day since then has been happier than the last. Not every day is perfect, but it's clear I've found a piece to my heart I didn't know I needed in Finley.

To top off all of that, tonight is my favorite night at the arena—Fanboni Night.

It's right after the first period, and I hop in my machine and crank on the engine. I have a girl waiting for me. Gripping the steering wheel a little tighter than normal, my stomach coils into knots of excitement as I glide forward onto the ice and set my sights on the line of fans, the first one being my biggest fan.

Finley's wearing her Granite Ice jersey, the one I got her that says Zamboni. It makes me smile when I think about how she never misses a game, even though I'm not a player. I pull to a stop right in front of the fan line, and the attendant gives her the nod to walk over. I don't wait for her to step up though. I have a different plan tonight. I step down from the machine and meet her right on the ice.

I'm all too aware of the Jumbotron above our heads, and it's likely zooming in on me. My palms wash with sweat as I will my mind to not let my nerves take over. I've been planning for this day for a while. Finley's eyes lock on mine, and her brow pins into a line of confusion. As I focus on her, the entire arena seems to fade, and the crowd's hums are drowned out by the sound of my heart beating in my throat. I take Finley's hand, and pause, looking deeply into her eyes.

She has a half smile on, as she scans the arena and then plants her gaze back on me. "What's going on? Aren't we going for a ride?" Then she drops her voice even more and whispers, "We're on the Jumbotron."

I don't have a speech. I'm not good with words, and the intermission is only so long. I swallow, pushing down my fears. "Finley," my voice cracks with vulnerability as I pull the modest diamond ring from my pocket. The crowd's hums immediately silence, and it's completely quiet.

Finley's eyes round, brimming with tears. Her hand flies to cover her mouth and I continue, "Today marks one year since we met, and it's been the best year of my life. I know we're young, and people say the odds are against us, but I don't care. I know with every ounce of my heart that I want to spend the rest of my life with you by my side."

This is it.

I gulp down the last of my stomach jitters and take a knee, as I pinch the ring between my forefinger and thumb with a death grip and hold it up to her. "I love you, Finley. Will you marry me?"

She's nodding before I even have the words out, and the crowd erupts into cheers. I can't hear a word she says. I take her nod as confirmation, and I slip the ring on her finger and pull her into a hug. She whispers, "Yes," into my ear, sending a shiver down my spine. I knew the crowd would go crazy, but this is unlike anything I've seen. There are so many whistles slicing the air when I lean down and drop a kiss on her lips, pulling back before it's anything more than sweet.

"I love you, Sam," Finley says as her gaze drifts to the ring on her finger and back to me.

I hold out my hand, as I have one thing left to do, and say, "It's time for our victory lap."

She slips her hand into mine, sending a shiver right to my heart. We climb aboard the Zamboni, which sets off another wave of cheers. We sit together, waving at the fans as I shift into gear, and pull forward, doing what I love to do the most, driving Finley.

Thank you for reading *Driving Miss Crazy*.

If you enjoy this sweet read, I'd be incredibly grateful if you took a moment to leave a review on Amazon or Goodreads. Your feedback not only helps others discover the book, but also means a lot to me personally as I'm able to see what you enjoyed about the story, and I can continue to make my stories better.

Acknowledgements

I'm not going to write a long post this time. I just want to say I love the sweet romance reader community. *You guys are all amazing.* Also, a huge thanks to my editing team (Karen and Rebecca). You ladies are saints for putting up with me.

And as always, thank you to my sweet little family and my Father in heaven, who has allowed me to steward this little platform.

Also by J.P. Sterling

<u>Christmas Shenanigans (All Standalones)</u>

Mingle All the Way

Tis the Season to Get Married

Let's Not and Sleigh We Did

<u>The Coffee Loft Series (All Standalones)</u>

Pardon My French Press

No More Mr. Chia Guy

Truly, Madly, Steeply Brew

<u>Sweet Hockey RomCom (All Standalones)</u>

The Pucker-Up Pact

Shot Through the Heart

Come and Get Your Glove

<u>Sweet Hockey RomCom Adjacent (Standalone)</u>

Driving Miss Crazy

<u>A Modern Fairy Tale Series (All Standalones)</u>

Royally Rugged

***Bosses and Billionaires Series* (All Standalones)**

Maid for my Billionaire Boss

Upcycling My Rig-Pig Boss

Kissed by My Billionaire Boss

Marooned with My Celebrity Boss

A Heart that Dances Series

Dancing on Broken Ankles

The Stars We See

A Heart that Dances

A Heart that Loves

Water and Stone Duet

Ruby in the Water

Lily in the Stone

About J.P. Sterling

J.P. Sterling grew up watching old reruns of Lucille Ball and Mary Tyler Moore and fell in love with wholesome entertainment and slapstick comedy. She loves leaning into the over-the-top humor and full circle moments, especially if it means the underdog gets to shine.

Aside from writing, she's also a wife and homeschooling mom, a holistic dietitian, a former college professor and lover of all-things dark chocolate.

*No swears. Just kisses. No Blasphemies. *

Let's get social!

Hey you amazing reader! You are invited to join my private reader group for all-things clean books and friends. Enter the group here: https://www.facebook.com/groups/happilyeverafterparty

Other places to follow me:

Instagram: https://www.instagram.com/stories/authorjpsterling/

Facebook: https://www.facebook.com/jpsterlingauthor/

www.ingramcontent.com/pod-product-compliance
Lightning Source LLC
Chambersburg PA
CBHW050416110726
47899CB00008B/2739